'It's what partners...

Nick gave a slight smile. 'I'd like to think we can be friends as well as partners. Don't you think we could at least give it a try?'

Friends! Somehow Beth felt it wasn't a word she would ever be able to apply to her feelings about Neil Quinn.

Almost as if he'd read her thoughts, he frowned and said softly, 'Is it really so difficult? Friends, Beth. That's all I'm asking . . .'

Jean Evans was born in Leicester and married shortly before her seventeenth birthday. She has two married daughters and several grandchildren. She gains valuable information and background for her medical romances from her husband, who is a senior nursing administrator. She now lives in Hampshire, close to the New Forest, and within easy reach of the historic city of Winchester.

Recent titles by the same author:

TAKE A CHANCE ON LOVE
A PRACTICE MADE PERFECT
HEART ON THE LINE
THE FRAGILE HEART

SOMEONE ELSE'S BABY

BY
JEAN EVANS

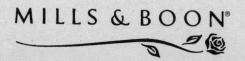

MILLS & BOON®

First published in Great Britain 1997
Harlequin Mills & Boon Limited,
Eton House, 18-24 Paradise Road, Richmond, Surrey TW9 1SR

© Jean Evans 1997

ISBN 0 263 80769 X

Set in Times 10 on 11½ pt. by
Rowland Phototypesetting Limited
Bury St Edmunds, Suffolk

03-9804-48530-D

Printed and bound in Great Britain
by Mackays of Chatham PLC, Chatham

CHAPTER ONE

'YES, George, and how often is she getting the contractions? Every twenty minutes? No, George, I wouldn't bother boiling kettles, unless you fancy a cup of tea. No... Yes, George, I think now is probably a good time to get Becky to the hospital. Yes, I know you're under a lot of stress, George, but, I promise you, Becky is going to be fine...'

Smiling, Dr Beth Maitland glanced at her watch and the cluttered surface of her desk. Evening surgery had been particularly hectic and she wasn't finished yet. Outside it was dark and the March wind carried a hint of fresh snow to come.

'I know Becky has had her case packed for a couple of weeks now. Just take a few things for the baby... No, George, toffees are not a good idea...'I'm not laughing at you, George. I know this is a worrying time for you, I appreciate that...'

Easing a strand of chestnut hair behind her ear, she tucked the phone under her chin and reached across the desk for the remains of a cup of coffee. 'Give her my love, George. Tell her I'll be thinking of her and I'll be in to see her as soon as she gets home.'

Moments later she put the phone down, rang the bell and looked up, smiling, as her next patient walked into the consulting room.

'Hello, Mrs Conroy. Take a seat and tell me what I can do for you.'

Mary Conroy was thirty-five. She looked pale and tired and uncomfortable. 'It's this backache, Doctor, and this sort of. . .burning sensation down here.' She pressed a hand gently across the lower area of her abdomen. 'It's been there for over a week now. I thought it might go away but. . .'

Beth nodded sympathetically. 'I take it it hasn't?'

The young woman smiled ruefully. 'If anything, I think it's slightly worse.'

Any problem with the waterworks?'

'Well, I do seem to be spending a penny rather more often than usual. Bill's getting grumpy because I keep waking him up when I get out of bed at night.'

A smile curved Beth's generous mouth. 'Any nausea? Temperature?'

Mary Conroy nodded. 'Both.'

Right.' Beth scanned the patient's notes and entered the information into the computer. 'I don't suppose you brought a urine specimen with you. . .?'

Mary handed over a small bottle, wrapped discreetly in a paper bag.

'Well done.' Beth rose to her feet, a tall, slim figure in a neat, knee-skimming grey skirt and silk blouse. 'I'm pretty sure you've got a bladder infection. I can do a quick test which will confirm it.'

Reaching into a cupboard, she produced a small jar from which she extracted a Clinitest strip and immersed it in the urine specimen.

'Yes, there we are—that's the villain of the piece. Right.' She disposed of the strip. 'Well, at least now I know what I'm dealing with I can give you something to make you feel more comfortable.' She printed out a prescription and handed it over. 'I'm giving you an antibiotic. Complete the whole course. You should feel much better in a few days. If not, come back and see me again.'

A few seconds later she saw her patient out and,

gathering up a batch of cards and notes, she carried them through to the reception area. 'Sorry to be so long with these. I had George Dawson on the phone. Becky's gone into labour—at last.'

The brown eyes of the practice manager, Ruth Baxter, twinkled. 'Poor man. How's he taking it?'

Making a rocking motion with her hand, Beth grinned. 'I think he'll survive—*just*. It's Becky I feel sorry for.'

'How much overdue is the baby?'

'Nearly three weeks.'

'Ouch!'

'Precisely.' Beth grinned. 'Still, a few hours from now it'll all be over. George will be a daddy.' She gave an exaggerated sigh. 'I'm not sure I can stand it.'

Chuckling, Ruth handed her a file. 'These are for signing. I'll get them off in the post tonight.'

'Fine.' Reaching for a pen, Beth scrawled her signature. 'I've got a couple of letters of referral here. No rush now—Monday will do. One's to Mr Carruther's.' She frowned. 'I want to get Peggy Atkins in to see him as soon as possible. She can't go on much longer with that hip of hers. And there's. . .ah, here we are. This one is to Mr Warren, the haematologist.'

'Over at Down Worthy General?'

'That's the one.' She riffled through the case notes. 'The results of Mr Douglas's blood tests have come back.' She frowned. 'I'm not happy about them. His platelet count is very low. I'd like to get him seen as soon as possible.' She straightened up, smiling, as she glanced across at Emma Stephens, the practice receptionist. 'Any more for me? Please say not.'

The blonde, twenty-five-year-old cupped her hand over the phone and grinned. 'You're off the hook. Mrs Conroy was the last.'

'Wonderful.' Beth glanced at the clock. 'Any sign of Alex yet?'

'He's still out on a call,' Emma mouthed. 'Right, Mr Davies, ten-thirty on Tuesday, then.' Putting down the phone, she scribbled a note in the diary. 'He had to go over to Athelmede. Old Mrs Tyson had a fall.'

Beth glanced anxiously at the leaden sky and shivered. 'From the looks of things, I'd say we're in for a lot more snow.' She glanced at Ruth. 'Are you off now?'

'I thought I would, if there's nothing else.' The older woman frowned, brushing a hand through her greying hair. 'Look, I feel awful, leaving you to it. . .'

'For heaven's sake, there's no need.' Beth smiled and waved as the slim, navy-clad figure of the practice nurse, Annie Collins, emerged from the treatment room, shrugging herself into her coat. 'See you on Monday.'

'Have a good weekend.'

'I should be so lucky.' Beth turned her attention back to the older woman. 'Look, you go. I know you've got your hands full at home right now. Anyway, it's my decision to stay late.'

'Well. . .if you're sure.'

'Absolutely.' She glanced at the window. 'Watch your step out there. It looks as if it's freezing.' Her words were confirmed as the door opened at that precise moment, wafting in a flurry of snow. 'I'll see you in the morning. Ah, speak of the devil. . .'

She turned to watch as Alex Thornton, the practice's senior partner, dropped his briefcase onto the desk, before blowing on his hands and heading for the radiator.

'Lor, it's cold out there.'

Anxiously, Beth surveyed his frozen features. 'How about some coffee?'

'Sounds like the best offer I've had all day.'

'Shall I. . .?' Emma hovered.

Smiling, Beth shook her head. 'I'll see to it. I'm staying on, anyway. You get off before you get snowed in.'

Heading for the small office, Beth flipped the switch on the electric kettle and spooned instant coffee and sugar into the cups. 'How's Mrs Tyson?' she called.

Alex Thornton frowned. A widower of sixty, white-haired and stockily built, he went to sit at the desk, brushing flakes of snow from his hair. 'Not so good. It's a broken hip this time. I got her admitted to hospital. She's not happy about it, mind.'

'No, I don't suppose she is.' Beth smiled wryly, pouring milk into the coffee and proffering the cup. 'How old is she now?'

'Eighty-two and sprightly as a bird.' Alex settled himself into his chair. 'The problem is getting her to accept her limitations.'

Shifting some papers, Beth sat on the edge of the desk and wrapped her hands round her own cup. 'It sounds as if she won't have any choice this time. Broken hips can be pretty dodgy in some older patients. What about her family? They don't live locally, do they?'

Alex stared unhappily at the papers on his desk. 'I think there's a son in Canada and a daughter somewhere in London. Hopefully, the hospital may be able to trace them. Whether it will make any difference. . .'

'It sounds as if you've done all you reasonably can.'

He frowned. 'Sometimes it seems precious little. If she makes it through this we'll have to have another go at trying to persuade her to consider warden accommodation. It's really the only safe answer if she wants to maintain her independence.'

Beth's mouth compressed as she nodded briefly.

'Sooner you than me. Maisie's a tough old girl and stubborn with it.'

'Don't I know it.' He gave a wry smile which didn't quite reach his eyes. 'Let's hope she's still around to make a fight of it. Anyway...' He drained his coffee and reached for his briefcase, snapping the locks. 'I think you wanted this.' He held up a shirt.

'You remembered!' Seizing it, Beth shrugged herself into the voluminous garment, rolling up the sleeves. It's length just skimmed the hem of her skirt. 'Alex, it's perfect. You're an angel.'

Alex Thornton's features assumed a pained expression. 'As long as you appreciate that I wouldn't hand over my favourite shirt to just anyone.'

She grinned. 'I promise I'll guard it with my life and you shall have it back afterwards, washed and pressed.'

He waved the suggestion away good-humouredly. 'It should have gone to the jumble sale years ago. Look, seriously, you don't have to stay behind to stack shelves, you know.'

'But I want to.' She hoisted a large cardboard box onto the table. 'We've waited two years for this new extension, Alex. You know how cramped things have been, with the practice expanding. The sooner we get it organised the sooner we'll stop falling over each other.'

'Well, I can't say I'm sorry to see the back of the builders. I just wish we could get rid of the smell of paint.'

'It'll fade, and it'll be worth it, you'll see.' Beth grinned. 'If I can stack most of the patients' record cards onto the shelves tonight—'

'Just in time to impress our latest applicant tomorrow.' Alex frowned. 'Let's hope he's better than the others. Better still that he actually *wants* to join us.'

He rose to his feet, digging his hands into his pockets.

'God knows, when Bob decided to move up north I knew we'd miss him. I just hadn't realised how difficult it would be to find a replacement. Things haven't exactly been easy on any of us this past three months, have they? What with the extra workload and the builders. . .'

'Oh, come on, Alex. We've managed.'

'"Managed" being the operative word.' He gave a slight smile. 'This is the worst time of year for us. Summer's bad enough, with all the summer visitors, but this latest flu epidemic has had people dropping like flies.' He pressed a hand briefly over hers.

'You've been doing a grand job—everyone has. But there's a limit to how much extra work we can carry and for how long, taking night calls and dealing with emergencies, and still take normal surgeries. We *need* an extra pair of hands.'

Beth looked at him keenly and was shocked to realise that suddenly—or maybe she simply hadn't seen it happening—he looked very tired, more than tired—exhausted.

Her throat tightened. 'We'll find someone, Alex. We're bound to. It's just taking time, that's all.'

'And time is the one luxury we don't have, not if we can even hope to function as efficiently as we should and the patients have a right to expect.' He gave a reluctant smile. 'Still, let's hope this latest applicant turns out to be the right one.'

'I'm sure he will be.' Anxious to ease his worries, she forced a note of confidence into her voice. 'His letter of application sounds very positive.'

Alex gave a short laugh. 'I'm beginning to realise that doesn't necessarily mean a thing. How many have we seen now? Four?'

'Five.' Stifling a sigh, Beth reached for the latest letter, scanning it for the umpteenth time.

Alex nodded. 'And each time we come up against the same problem. Wadeley is a small seaside town so either they think we're too far off the beaten track or they see us as a stepping stone, a temporary stop-over, on the way to somewhere bigger and more permanent.' He raked a hand through his hair. 'We have to find someone who's prepared to settle in the area.'

Frowning, Beth flipped the page and scanned the information listed there. 'Previous experience. . .' She sighed heavily. 'I can't help thinking this one sounds almost too good to be true. Why would anyone want to move from the city, especially someone with qualifications like these, to a place like Wadeley?'

'I don't know, but let's not look a gift horse in the mouth. The interview is arranged for tomorrow, by the way.'

'Yes, I know. But why Saturday? It's a bit unusual, isn't it?'

Alex glanced at his watch, dropped a couple of case notes into his briefcase and closed it. 'I know it's short notice, but it happens to fit in with Dr Quinn's travel arrangements and work schedule. Besides, if he does turn out to be the man for the job, the sooner the better.' He headed for the door. 'Thanks for the coffee. I've got a couple more calls to make, then I'm off home. Are you sure you'll be all right?'

'I'll be fine.' She followed him to the door and saw him out with a smile, before turning and making her way briskly back to the office. 'Oh, well, here goes.'

Sweeping her hair deftly into a ponytail and securing it with an elastic band, she hauled the stepladder firmly into place, reached for the first batch of cards and hitched her straight, tailored skirt above her knees. 'I just hope you appreciate all the effort, Dr Neil Quinn, whoever you are,' she muttered, hanging on grimly as the ladder swayed precariously.

She hummed softly to herself as gradually the bright new shelves began to fill with patients' record cards.

She reflected on the fact that over the past few years she had seen the practice flourish and expand to fill the needs of a busy community, swelled in summer by the arrival of tourists and in winter because of the town's popularity as a retirement area. Unfortunately, the size of the surgery hadn't kept pace with demand.

Yes, she thought with a nod of satisfaction as she eased her way unsteadily up the ladder yet again, life was certainly going to be easier with the completion of the new and larger office and an extension to the waiting room.

Hauling the oversized, borrowed shirt out of the way, she stretched to tuck a bundle of cards into the remaining space on the top shelf. It was an ambitious move, she realised as the ladder rocked and, with a small yelp, she shot out a hand to steady herself.

'Aren't you being just a shade irresponsible?' came a distinctly gravelly male voice, making her jump so that the ladder rocked even more precariously.

Holding onto the shelf with a grim effort as she steadied herself, she turned her head slowly and found herself staring into a pair of startlingly blue eyes. The breath momentarily snagged in her throat. It was shock, she told herself, and wondered how long he had been standing there, watching her struggle. Why hadn't she heard the outer door?

Releasing one hand tentatively to blow the stray tendrils of chestnut hair from her eyes, she took a longer look at the intruder and almost wished she hadn't. It was an unnerving experience.

He was tall, over six feet. That much she could judge, even from her unsteady position and those blue eyes seemed to be directed far too appreciatively at her knees.

His face was strong, ruggedly chiselled. His hair was dark, matching the growth of what she decided was designer stubble on his chin. He looked at the same time faintly disreputable and very dangerously male, and his unannounced presence in the small office was beginning to have a definitely unsettling effect on her nervous system.

She edged one foot unsteadily towards the lower step, muttering under her breath.

'Not exactly dressed for it, are you?' the man remarked, his gaze lingering with undisguised interest on her black-stockinged leg.

'What?' she snapped uncharitably, tugging at her skirt in a futile attempt to thwart the blatantly lingering gaze. 'How did you get in? I thought the door was locked.'

Powerful shoulders moved as slowly he eased down the zip of his black leather jacket. 'Apparently not. I just walked straight in.' The glittering gaze narrowed. 'Are you alone?'

'Not for long.' Her voice sounded strangely husky. She certainly wasn't about to volunteer that sort of information to a stranger. For all she knew, he could be a burglar. . .or worse! She frowned. 'I was sure I locked that door.' She juggled a large cardboard box and the ladder swayed again.

'Perhaps I can help.' A smile tugged at his mouth. 'Here, let me.'

'No, thank you, I'm fine.' She again eased one foot slowly downwards. 'I don't need any—' The ladder swayed, and the box fell. Her foot somehow missed the step, and a pair of strong hands caught her round the waist in a firm grip. Her fingers made contact with tautly muscled arms.

'It's all right. I've got you.' He moved back slowly, taking her with him. For several seconds, it seemed, she was suspended effortlessly in mid-air, then he lowered her slowly, sliding her down his long, leather-clad body until her feet finally touched the floor. It was a journey that seemed to go on for ever—until she came to rest somewhere on a level with his chest.

'There we are—a perfect touch-down. You're quite safe, but should you really be doing this sort of thing in your condition?'

'Condition?' she repeated, her mind strangely confused and a small line furrowing her brow.

'If you must climb ladders, not that I recommend it. . .' blue eyes quizzed her in a way that made her feel anything but safe '. . .I strongly advise you to wear more sensible shoes. Better still, get someone else to do the mountain goat bit—at least for the time being.'

'What. . .?' The line etched itself deeper. For some strange reason her brain didn't seem to be functioning properly.

One dark eyebrow rose. 'Aren't you taking unnecessary risks? I'm surprised, especially working in a place like this.'

'Risks?' The mists clogging her brain cleared. Realisation dawned and she yelped as though she had been scalded. The shirt she had borrowed from Alex had made him think she was pregnant!

'Don't be ridiculous,' she snapped edgily. 'I'm not married.'

He released her slowly. 'It's all right. I'm pretty broad-minded,' he said, his voice a pleasant baritone. The amazingly sensuous mouth moved. 'I imagine most people are these days. All the same, should you really be taking risks?'

His head tilted back, his blue gaze wandering with lazy appreciation over her—from her chestnut hair, caught back in its ponytail, down along the curve of her hips to her legs in the slender-heeled shoes.

The subtle fragrance of his aftershave remained, filling her nostrils and mingling with his own warm, male scent.

Her mouth tightened as she unbuttoned the shirt, flinging it over the back of a chair.

'Ah.' But the smile didn't fade one jot. 'So, what, then? Drugs? Is that it? You're looking for drugs. I'm afraid you'll probably be disappointed.' He leaned casually against the doorjamb. 'Help is available, you know, for people with a habit.'

'Don't be ridiculous,' she said testily. 'Do I look like an addict?'

Blue eyes studied her for a long and very disturbing moment. 'Who knows? They come in all shapes and sizes, and I dare say an unlocked door might have been too much of a temptation.'

He moved away from her and began to wander round the room, letting his glance flit in a desultory fashion over the freshly emulsioned walls and the half-filled shelves that adorned them.

'You still haven't explained what you're doing here. Perhaps I can help?' she suggested, deliberately keeping her tone even.

'Coffee would be nice.'

Beth choked. Briskly she mentally slapped down any notion that she might be about to offer hospitality, even if he did look as if he needed it. Her gaze edged towards the jar of instant coffee and the kettle, then away again. 'We don't do coffee,' she said churlishly.

He rasped the back of his hand across the designer stubble. 'I was afraid you might say that.'

She refused to be swayed by the winsome smile. 'If it's coffee you're after wouldn't you have done better to go to a café?'

He reached out to straighten a fallen file, righting it on the shelf. 'Probably,' he muttered. 'I just didn't get around to it. I was rather hoping to see Dr Thornton.'

She blinked hard. 'You had an appointment?'

'Well, no. Not exactly.'

'In that case, I'm sorry to disappoint you but you've had a wasted journey. Surgery finished over an hour ago. Surgery hours are clearly displayed on the notice-board by the entrance.'

'I thought there might just be a chance he would be working late.' His attention was diverted by a row of medical textbooks, and Beth observed him with grow-ing irritation as he reached for one, flicking idly through the pages.

'Dr Thornton had to go out on a call,' she said bluntly. 'You could have saved yourself a journey if you'd rung earlier.'

'You're right, of course.' He snapped the book closed, replaced it and fixed her with a speculative regard. 'Do you usually work so late?'

Her own gaze flickered and she experienced a fresh sense of panic. Watching him warily, she chewed at her lip. She didn't know this man from Adam. He had simply wandered in from the street. He could be *any-one*. However, she noticed that even though his jeans were faded they were of good quality. Perhaps he had to resort to burglary to fund his expensive tastes!

'No, I. . .er. . .not usually. Look, can I help? If you need to see a doctor. . .' She glanced at the phone. If only she could get help from Alex—someone, *anyone*.

With an effort she managed to smile. 'Perhaps I could call Dr Thornton. He's probably home by now.'

She reached for the phone but he lazily intercepted her, his hand resting over the phone.

'No, don't bother. I'll catch up with him soon enough. I'll be in the area for a while.'

Sleeping rough, no doubt. Seen close to, he did look decidedly the worse for wear, she noticed. His dark hair was just a shade too long, curling against his collar.

He dug his hands in his pockets. 'Still, my journey wasn't entirely wasted. At least we had a chance to become acquainted.' He quirked an eyebrow at her and she felt an odd, fluttering sensation somewhere in her ribcage.

Indigestion, she told herself. Too much coffee.

He strolled towards the door, then paused. An indulgent smile showed his even white teeth. He was really quite attractive in a rugged sort of way, she decided. Not her type, of course, but she could see why some women might fall for the dark good looks.

Until now she hadn't noticed the tiny lines of tiredness that edged his mouth, but they were there, adding a hint of ruthlessness which left her feeling momentarily shaky.

'It might be a good idea in future to keep the door locked. You never know who might stroll in and take advantage.'

Colour flooded her cheeks as with a start she realised he was returning her gaze. She pressed her lips together and held the door open. 'I'll do that.' She was about to close it behind him, shivering in the sudden blast of cold air, when he paused.

'What now?' Beth began tetchily, resenting the firm hand which seemed to close effortlessly over hers.

One dark eyebrow rose. 'I don't suppose you could direct me to the nearest pub?'

'You'll find the Horse and Jockey a couple of miles along the coast road,' she advised him sharply. 'On the other hand, if you're really desperate you could try the Pig and Parrot.'

'I'll do that.' He sketched a salute.

She watched him as he headed for the outer door. Sympathy vied with natural caution. He did look decidedly the worse for wear. Perhaps he couldn't afford to eat.

On impulse, she reached for her bag and, with a jerky movement, extracted a ten-pound note. She thrust it into his hand and saw him gaze at it in a kind of bewildered wonderment.

'For me?' An odd, choking sound came from his throat. 'I don't know what to say.'

It was probably more money than he had seen in a month, she thought, sanity rapidly returning. What was she doing, handing out money to a down-and-out? Given the slightest encouragement, he would probably be back tomorrow for more.

'Just don't imagine for one minute that I make a habit of this sort of thing,' she said decisively.

He grunted. 'I wouldn't dream of it.'

'I suggest you get yourself something to eat and drink. Something warm and *non-alcoholic*.'

His jaw clenched perceptibly as he considered her briefly from beneath ridiculously thick lashes. 'I don't suppose you'd care to join me in a cheese sandwich? I'm sure we could make it stretch to two. You look pretty skinny. I shouldn't think you'd cost much to keep.'

'*Out!*' Beth snapped, wrenching open the door. 'You'll find the pub about half a mile from here.' Not nearly far enough—the thought lingered to frustrate her as he sketched another salute and sauntered out onto the pavement.

It was raining—hard. Good, she thought uncharitably.

'Oh, and perhaps you'd tell Dr Thornton I called?' His voice reached her through the growing darkness just as she was about to close the door.

And how was she supposed to do that, she wondered, when she didn't even know his name? She peered out into the street. It was empty, apart from a car which suddenly roared off into the distance.

Shaking her head, she turned away, closed the door and firmly locked it. A girl couldn't be too careful. There were some very strange people about.

CHAPTER TWO

'MORNING,' Ruth Baxter trilled as she replaced the phone, making a note before she glanced up with a smile at Beth. 'You did a good job on those shelves last night. I think we're beginning to get there at last. It actually looks like a new office.'

'It is rather nice, isn't it?' With an answering smile, Beth dragged off her gloves, before peering over the desk at the duty list. 'Any for me?'

'One call—from Mr West. His wife says he's a bit chesty. She'd be grateful if you could pop over to take a look at him some time today, if you can manage it.'

'Will do.' Beth hung up her coat, before turning to sort through the stack of morning mail. 'The usual exciting stuff, I see.'

Ruth grinned. 'At least the waiting room is empty. Let's be grateful for small mercies, shall we?' Saturday morning surgery was for emergencies only—except that they both knew things didn't always work out that way.

'The snow must be putting people off.' Beth tossed aside the letters. 'Is Alex in yet?'

The phone began to ring again. Reaching for it, Ruth cupped a hand over the receiver. 'In his office. Good morning, Wadeley Surgery. . .'

Beth left the older woman to it, and made her way along the corridor to Alex's consulting room. The door was open and he was seated at the desk, his jacket slung over the back of his chair.

'Hi.' She smiled. 'You're an early bird.'

'Thought I'd catch on a bit of paperwork while I had the chance.' He stared unhappily at the papers on his desk. 'I seem to be fighting a losing battle. I'm beginning to think the stuff breeds overnight.'

Beth grinned. 'I know the feeling. By the way, have you heard? Becky Dawson had her baby late last night. A girl. Seven pounds five ounces. I've said I'll go over to see her as soon as she gets home.'

'How did it go? I know you were slightly worried about her blood pressure towards the end.'

'Everything was fine. No complications. Well, apart from the fact that George passed out.'

Alex chuckled. 'Poor George. I think he's had a harder time through this pregnancy than Becky. So, we'll be adding another name to our lists, I suppose.'

'Looks like it. I'm just so glad for them that it worked out so happily. I think they'd almost given up all hope of having a baby. In fact, I think if that second try at the IVF treatment hadn't worked they would have.' She frowned. 'Adoption isn't every childless couple's alternative choice, is it?'

'It isn't always an option.'

'No,' she shook her head. 'I appreciate that. Age can be against some couples.' She pushed a stray wisp of hair behind her ear. 'I suppose when the Maitlands adopted me it was easier because they were prepared to take a toddler rather than a baby.'

Alex looked at her. 'I still forget you were adopted.'

She smiled slightly. 'So do I sometimes. Still, as far as the practice is concerned, one extra little patient won't make too much difference, will it? Especially as we're hopefully going to have an extra pair of hands around the place. Talking of which. . .' she glanced, frowning, at her watch '. . .what time is Dr Quinn due to arrive?'

'He got here a short time ago. He was early so I got Ruth to put him in Bob's old consulting room with a large pot of coffee. Apparently, he's quite happy, reading magazines.'

'At least he seems keen.' She stifled a sigh. 'Let's hope it lasts longer than the duration of the interview.'

Alex sat up, his eyes twinkling as he dropped his pen onto the desk. 'Where's your spirit of optimism?'

'It walked out of the door, along with the last applicant.' She grinned, then sobered. 'Seriously, Alex, I'm beginning to feel just a shade desperate. I mean, what do we have to do. . .?'

'I know.' He pressed her hand briefly. 'But let's look on the bright side. At least this one has turned up and, as far as I know, he's still waiting to be interviewed. So. . .what say we get to it before he changes his mind. The sooner we do it the sooner we'll know. I'll go and fetch him, shall I?'

Her chin lifted and with an effort she forced a smile to her lips. 'You're right. Let's do it. Give me a minute to tidy myself up. Where shall we see him? Your room or mine?'

'Yours.' He grinned. 'It's tidier and you have flowers.'

'With our luck, he'll be allergic.' She laughed and made her way along the corridor, pausing briefly in Reception to drop off a signed repeat prescription at the desk. 'Can you see that Mrs Walker gets this if she calls in?' she said to Ruth. 'I said I'd have it ready for her so that she can start the antibiotics over the weekend.'

Heading for her consulting room, she glanced into the small play area. Usually on Saturdays it would be empty.

On this occasion, however, a small boy of about

five years old, dressed in sturdy jeans and a slightly
over-large sweater, was lying sprawled on the floor
with a set of large colourful crayons and a sheet of
paper, busily drawing a picture. He'd probably come in
with his mother and had been left to play, she thought.

Pausing in the doorway, she smiled. 'Hello, there.
Are you all right? Is someone looking after you?'

He turned his head to gaze at her, waving the sheet
of paper in her direction. 'I'm drawing a picture of
Daddy. Look.'

Beth caught a glimpse of the colourful drawing of a
stick-like figure with a thatch of what was clearly supposed to be a thatch of unruly black hair, and found
herself suppressing a grin.

'That's wonderful. I'm sure he'll be very pleased.'

The child studied the drawing earnestly, before adding a splash of brilliant red. 'He's going to buy me an
ice cream if I'm a good boy.'

Well, good for Daddy, Beth thought. What's a little
bribery and corruption between friends? He's obviously
played this game before.

Opening a cupboard, she pulled out a large box.
'Here we are. Why don't you have a look through these
while you're waiting? I'm sure there'll be something
in there you might like to play with.'

'Racing cars!' he exclaimed, his wide-eyed gaze
drinking in the selection of colourful toys as he pulled
them out one by one.

'Enjoy your ice cream.' Beth waved as she made her
way across the corridor to her own consulting room
where she eyed the vase of chrysanthemums on her
desk, shifting it to the top of the nearby filing cabinet.
Shaking her head, she put it back in its original spot.

'Let's face it, if he's put off by a bunch of flowers
then he's not right for us anyway,' she conceded aloud,

flicking a comb briskly through her hair and adding a touch of lipstick to her mouth. 'Right, Dr Neil Quinn. . .' she nodded at her reflection in the small mirror '. . .let's be having you, then. Coming, ready or not.'

Alex tapped at the door. 'Here we are. Let me introduce you. Beth, this is Dr Quinn. Dr Quinn—my partner, Beth Maitland.'

She turned with a smile on her face, her hand outstretched. 'Dr Quinn, I'm del—' Her smile froze as she stood, feeling the shock waves engulf her. It was *him*. Her down-and-out of the previous evening. She closed her eyes briefly as realisation dawned, telling herself it was all part of a bad dream. But when she opened them again he was still there, admittedly clean-shaven now but there, nonetheless.

'Dr Maitland. I'd like to say it's a real pleasure.'

Had she imagined it or had there been just the slightest emphasis on the word 'like'?

Her smile was rigid with suppressed anger as his blue eyes regarded her with an unreadable expression. Only the slightest tremor at the corner of his mouth suggested that he was enjoying himself enormously at her expense.

She had to resist the urge to run for cover as he held her hand in a firm grip, smiling with all the charm of a panther stalking its prey.

'Dr Quinn.'

'Dr Maitland.' His hand took hers, and instinctively she tried to pull away. The pressure of his fingers was firm and male and very unsettling, and she felt warm colour flood into her cheeks.

'Please, call me Neil. I hope we're going to get to know each other much better.'

Her teeth grated on a smile as she released her hand

from his grasp. His voice was a soft, tantalising drawl, and she wished she could back away from the smell of expensive aftershave which was stirring up memories she would far rather forget. Mentally she shook herself. She wasn't about to give him the satisfaction of seeing that she was in the least bothered by him.

'Welcome to Wadeley, Dr Quinn.' She moved briskly aside and indicated a seat, placing herself firmly at the other side of the desk. 'I take it you didn't have any trouble finding us.'

'None at all.' He sat, nonchalantly crossing his long legs. 'People can be so friendly and helpful, don't you find?'

She choked on a reply, conscious of Alex fixing her with a troubled frown as he settled into his own chair.

'Perhaps we can get on,' Alex said. He dropped a buff file onto the desk, extracting several pages from it. 'I don't want to rush things, but I do have a couple of calls to make and I'm sure you'll be wanting to get back to London.' He looked at his watch. 'You must have started out pretty early.'

'Oh, I travelled up yesterday evening. It made sense.' Neil Quinn gave a slight laugh. 'I'd been on emergency call. You know how it is. I had to see a patient at five in the morning. By the time I got home it was hardly worth going back to bed so I did my surgery, threw some things in to a bag and came up here.'

Glancing up, Beth found herself staring into the thickly lashed eyes—disturbingly blue eyes which, at that moment, were filled with a sardonic amusement that made her pulse quicken even as her own grey eyes flashed with annoyance.

'You should have given us a call.' Alex poured coffee from the tray Ruth had thoughtfully provided, handing

the cups round. 'At least we could have offered hospitality—done something to entertain you.'

Blue eyes slanted in Beth's direction as Neil Quinn
sipped at the hot, dark liquid, and she had the distinct
impression that he was laughing at her. 'It was
rather late.'

'Even so. . .'

Draining the dregs of her own coffee, Beth pushed
the cup away, only to feel Neil Quinn's fingers brush
against hers as he rose slowly to his feet to take it
from her.

The ghost of a smile touched his mouth, as though
he read her uneasy thoughts.

'Oh, I can assure you, I was very well taken care
of,' he drawled softly.

He was tall and slim and muscular, and once again
she was immediately conscious of every line of his
body—from the taut shoulders to the slender waist and
lean thighs beneath the dark grey trousers he was
wearing.

With a determined effort, she dragged her gaze up
to meet his, saying briskly, 'Yes, well, perhaps we
should get on. I'm sure we wouldn't want to keep you
since you have a long journey ahead of you.'

'Ready whenever you are.' He returned to his chair,
his eyes narrowed as if to mock what he knew to be
an air of assumed self-confidence as he made himself
comfortable, stretching his long legs out in front of
him. 'Where would you like to start?'

'Perhaps you'd like to tell us a bit about yourself.'
Alex was studying a sheaf of papers. 'I see you trained
at St Benedict's.'

'Yes, that's right.'

'It's one of the best.'

'I think so.' A smile curved the generous mouth. 'But, then, I may be biased.'

'You did a year in surgery?'

'Yes, I decided it wasn't for me. Too impersonal somehow.'

'Mmm, I can understand that. So you decided, finally, on general practice.'

'I prefer the more personal touch, meeting people on a one-to-one basis.'

'Well I think we can both relate to that, don't you, Beth?'

With an effort she forced a smile to her lips. 'I suppose we're lucky. Wadeley is a tightly knit community. The people are friendly.' She shot him a look and saw a nerve pulse in his jaw.

Alex reached for one of the papers, frowning. 'I see you spent some time with VSO in. . .' He flicked the page.

'Africa. Yes, that's right. I was out there for twelve months.'

'It must have been quite an experience.'

'Yes, it was.'

'Would you care to tell us about it?'

Beth stared out of the window. It was snowing again, just a few light flakes.

'I was part of a team, sent out to set up a small outpatients clinic and to carry out an immunisation programme. The area had become a sort of unofficial camp for refugees, bringing with it all the attendant problems, mostly disease.'

'Measles, I suppose?'

'Measles, tuberculosis, polio. You name it, they had it—on a scale I've never seen before and wouldn't much care to see again.'

'I'm afraid we have very little to offer in the way of

excitement here in Wadelely, Dr Quinn.' Beth turned and felt her throat tighten as for a few seconds she became aware of those shrewd blue eyes meeting hers.

'This is a relatively quiet community, with a preponderance of elderly people. Don't you think you might find it a little too quiet? Why would you want to leave a large city practice to come to a small seaside town?'

He smiled and, to her annoyance, her heart gave an odd little leap. 'It seems, from what I've seen of it, to be a nice healthy town. Healthy as in thriving and in clean air. Plenty of schools, shops, churches—'

'And pubs,' she muttered uncharitably.

Blue eyes glinted. 'As you say.' His mouth tightened.

'I've been part of the rat race. Things are changing fast and I don't particularly like what's happening. Oh, I'm not saying it's all bad, but medicine is losing its caring face. It's becoming big business and I get the feeling that the overriding factor is money, rather than people's lives. Frankly, Dr Maitland, I decided it's a price I'm no longer prepared to pay.'

Beth shifted uneasily as his words seemed to echo something of her own thoughts. Wadeley was a beautiful small seaside town, but in the past couple of years even here she had seen subtle changes taking place.

'I suppose I can understand that,' she conceded. 'But I hope you don't imagine that because Wadelely is a small town it will be a sinecure. Believe me, it won't.'

Alex shot her a curious look and she had the grace to blush.

'I just wouldn't want anyone to get the wrong idea.'

Neil Quinn drawled softly, 'Perish the thought.'

Her chin lifted. 'You don't think you might find it a little tame after what you're used to?'

'On the contrary.' Humour tinged his voice. 'From the little I've seen so far, I'd say it has a lot to offer.'

Damn the man! Couldn't he take a hint? The colour rose in her cheeks but she was saved from having to make a response as Alex intervened, seemingly blithely unaware of any tension.

'Well, I'm delighted you think so,' he enthused. 'Beth's right. This time of year things are pretty quiet but, come the summer, they can get fairly hectic once the tourists descend. The practice is actually expanding.'

'I noticed there's quite a lot of building going on in the area.'

Alex suppressed a sigh. 'Overspill areas. Still, I suppose we shouldn't complain. As Beth said, for the main part of the year Wadeley is a retirement area, which means we see a lot of older patients.'

'That isn't so very different from what I've been used to.'

Alex was on his feet, smiling. 'So you really feel you might like to join us?'

'I'd like that very much. When had you in mind?'

'The sooner the better, I think, don't you?' He glanced smilingly at Beth.

She took a long, hard look at Dr Neil Quinn. As he rose to his feet an indulgent smile showed even, white teeth. She decided that he was really quite attractive, in a rugged sort of way.

'Don't you agree, Beth?' Colour flooded her cheeks as with a start she jerked back to the realisation that she was being addressed by Alex.

'I. . .I'm sorry?'

'Neil was saying that his present contract is officially ended so there's no reason why he shouldn't start a week on Monday. That's great news, isn't it?'

'Oh, absolutely. Yes.' Her jaw clenched perceptibly.

'But won't you need a little more time to organise things?'

'There isn't a great deal to organise. My flat is at the end of its lease. Besides, I'd like to get Jamie settled. Things haven't exactly been easy for him so far.'

Her head jerked up. 'Jamie?'

'My son,' he said evenly. 'He's five. He started school a few months ago.'

Beth felt her heart give an extra thud. She realised it hadn't even occurred to her that he might be married. 'I'm so sorry. I had no idea. But won't he find it all a bit of an upheaval, moving from the city to a place like Wadeley?'

'He'll probably see it all as something of an adventure.' Neil straightened up and she saw the cool amusement in his eyes. 'In my experience, children are amazingly resilient.'

She felt slightly chastened, realising that she had jumped to several hasty conclusions where he was concerned. It was almost a relief when Ruth tapped at the door and popped her head round.

'Sorry to disturb you, Alex. There's a call for you. Young Katie Wilson. Her mum's worried about her.'

Alex frowned. 'Tell her I'm on my way.' He was on his feet, already reaching for his briefcase. To Neil he said, 'Sorry about this, but the child's an asthmatic and the mother isn't the sort to call the surgery unless she's genuinely worried.'

'It's all right. I quite understand.'

Alex dropped the card Ruth had placed on the desk into his briefcase. He reached for his coat, shrugging himself into it, then smilingly proffered his hand. 'So, let's make it official, then, shall we? If you want the job it's yours.'

'In that case, I'm delighted to accept.'

The two men shook hands. 'Welcome to Wadeley.'

There was no mistaking Alex's satisfaction as he said it.

'Welcome to the practice, Dr Quinn. I hope you're going to enjoy working with us.' Beth offered her own hand, conscious of the blue eyes appraising her with mocking amusement.

'The name is Neil, and I'm sure it will be an experience, Dr Maitland.'

She wondered what his wife was like. The thought was oddly disturbing and she released her hand sharply to make an exaggerated play of gathering up her own coat and briefcase.

'I don't suppose you've had time to think about accommodation?' Alex paused in the doorway.

'I'm sure it won't be a problem. I'll find something on a temporary basis. I noticed there's a small hotel locally. It will do until I can get settled.'

'Hmm. Hardly satisfactory, though, is it? Not with a family.' Alex frowned. 'Look, there's a house going begging—on a temporary basis, anyway. It belongs to our previous partner, Bob Scott, and his wife, Barbara, who lived there until they decided to move up north. It's available to rent, at least until they decide what their future plans are. Might be worth considering.'

'I'll certainly do that. It sounds ideal.'

'Well, I'm sure Beth will be delighted to take you over there, fill you in on the details and show you around. Won't you, my dear?'

'Well, I. . .'

'Good, good.' Alex beamed. 'In that case, I'll see you a week on Monday. In the meantime, I'll leave you in Beth's capable hands. I'm sure she'll look after you.'

'I'm sure she will.' Neil Quinn's voice was pleasantly silky.

She chose to ignore his sarcasm. Glancing at her watch, she headed for the door. 'Well, Dr Quinn, I won't keep you. I'm sure you'll be wanting to get back. If you'll let me know when you'd like to see the house, I have a key.'

Blue eyes glinted as he consulted his own watch. 'I take it you don't have surgery?' As she shook her head he went on, 'In that case, there's no time like the present. Shall we go?' He stood aside, waiting for her to pass.

With an effort, Beth forced a smile to her lips as she fumbled for her keys. 'You'd like to see it *now?*'

'It makes sense, don't you think? We'll take my car, shall we? Unless you prefer yours?'

She jumped as his hand came beneath her elbow. In a small, nervous gesture she moistened her lips with her tongue. 'Well, I—'

'Good. In that case, I'll just collect Jamie and we can be off.'

She stared at him. 'Y—you mean your son is here?'

'In the waiting room.' His dark brows drew together. 'Unfortunately, I had no choice but to bring him with me. My sitter let me down. Still, as it turned out, it was probably for the best. At least he's seen something of the area and the practice.'

Beth could feel herself blushing again. 'But. . .last night. . .'

His mouth twisted. 'A very nice policeman stood guard over Jamie in the car while I popped into the surgery. Later we found a very nice pub, thank you very much. The landlord fed us handsomely, then found us a very nice room. So, you see, I'm very grateful to you, Dr Maitland. Now, shall we go?'

'Daddy! I've done a drawing of you,' Jamie announced, coming to wave a large sheet of paper in front of his father's face as they walked into Reception. 'And the lady gave me some cars to play with.'

Neil Quinn studied the colourful drawing and swept his son up in his arms. 'Well, that's great, tiger.' He raised one eyebrow. 'I think maybe it's time I got a haircut, though, don't you?'

He glanced at Beth. 'I gather you've already met, but perhaps I'd better make the introductions, anyway. Jamie, this is Dr Maitland. Beth, this is Jamie.'

Blue heavily lashed eyes, so like his father's, locked with hers and Beth felt as if someone had reached out and tugged at her heart. So this was Neil's son. Pale and fair-haired, so unlike him in looks and yet, without any shadow of doubt, his. She could only guess that Jamie must take after his mother, in which case she must be beautiful.

Very solemnly they shook hands. 'Hello, Jamie.'

'Hello, Dr Maitland,' came the shy response.

'Please.' She smiled. 'I'm sure we're going to be good friends so why don't you call me Beth? That is. . .' she glanced up '. . .if your daddy doesn't mind.'

His gaze narrowed briefly. 'I don't see why not, if you're happy with that.' He held his son's hand. 'The nice lady is going to show us a house. How about that?'

Jamie laughed as his father swung him up onto his shoulders. 'Yes, let's go. And then can I have my ice cream?'

Neil gave a mock groan. Beth grinned, murmuring softly, 'You didn't imagine you were going to get away with it, did you, Dr Quinn?' More loudly she said, 'I think a giant-sized, double scoop with nuts and syrup sounds about right, don't you?'

'*Yes!*' Jamie applauded.

'Oh, great.' Neil shot her a look. 'I can see whose side you're on.'

Moments later they were heading out into the cold air.

Neir had a large, modern car. Even so, she was still aware of him, too close. She could smell the distinctive, musky aftershave he was wearing as she climbed reluctantly into the passenger seat and, with Jamie strapped securely into the rear seat, they set off. She purposely averted her eyes, concentrating on the passing, frost-whitened hedgerows.

'I'm grateful to you for taking the time to show us the house. I realise you probably have far better things to do with your weekend.'

Her head jerked up and she felt her throat tighten as for a few seconds she became aware of the blue eyes meeting hers.

'It's no problem. I'm sorry I didn't think to ask if you were married. You should have let us know. We could have been better prepared.'

'I didn't realise it mattered.' Humour tinged his voice as he took his gaze briefly from the road. 'I'm sorry you're not happy about me joining the practice.'

Beth looked at him sharply. 'I didn't say that.'

'You didn't have to.' His dark brows drew together. 'We didn't exactly get off to the best of starts, did we?'

'I wonder whose fault that was?' she snapped, moving as far away from him as possible.

'I may have jumped to some rather hasty conclusions. . .' Blue eyes regarded her with an unreadable expression. Only the slight tremor at the corner of his mouth suggested that he was amused. 'Do you think we could start all over again? Just tell me what I have to do. I'm quite prepared to eat any amount of humble pie.'

Now she knew he was laughing at her and, for some reason, she felt herself respond with a faint smile. Perhaps she was being a little childish, bearing a grudge towards someone who, after all, knew nothing about her and, more to the point, was going to be the answer to a prayer—as far as the practice went.

'Maybe we both jumped to conclusions,' she conceded.

'I suppose I could have been more helpful, tried to explain. If there's anything you need to know. . .'

'It's not important,' she countered briskly. Some things, like Pandora's box, were best left undisturbed. 'We got off to a bad start. Let's just leave it at that, shall we?'

His mouth twisted. 'Should we kiss and make up, do you think?'

Beth looked at him sharply. 'I suggest you just keep your eyes on the road, Doctor, and don't push your luck.'

It was almost a relief when they drew up at the roadside and she was able to climb out of the car to gaze up at the large, stone-built house. It was set back from the road, with a driveway and steps leading to the front. To the rear, glimpsed through a side-gate, were several old trees and a small enclosed paddock.

'The Scotts kept a couple of ponies for the girls. They have two daughters,' she explained. 'Right now, the neighbours have permission to keep their goat and a couple of rabbits on the land.'

'Rabbits! Hooray!' With a whoop of delight, Jamie was away through the gate and into the paddock.

Smiling wryly, Neil closed the car door and came to stand beside her, then followed, hands in pockets, as she unlocked the front door and went in.

Inside he stood in silence as his gaze swept from the large, open fireplace to the modern furnishings.

'It's quite large. I'm not sure how many rooms you need,' she said anxiously. 'I'm afraid it's quite chilly, although the neighbour does come in regularly to light a fire and check the central heating.'

'It's very nice,' he murmured, moving to the window to stare out at the surrounding fields.

Beth crossed to one of the doors. 'The kitchen is through here. It's quite large.' Probably just as well, she thought. A six-foot-and-then-some man in a tiny kitchen could be a problem—in more ways than one. She averted her eyes. 'I think you'll find everything you're likely to need. If not, I dare say we could come to some arrangement.'

'Don't worry about it.' He gave a slight and surprisingly attractive smile. 'The microwave and I are well acquainted, and I imagine there's a tin opener somewhere around.'

His wife must be working full time as well, then, Beth thought.

'The bedrooms are up here.' She led the way upstairs, pushing open the first door. 'The girls shared this room.' It was prettily furnished, with twin beds, matching carpet and curtains.

Neil nodded.

'And this is the largest room.' Again, Barbara Scott's eye for colour and design was in evidence. The furnishings and curtains had been chosen to create maximum effect, creating an illusion of space in which the centrepiece was a large bed. She tore her eyes from it to find Neil watching her. 'I. . .don't know what more I can tell you.'

He frowned. 'Why would the Scotts want to leave a place like this empty?'

She followed him down the stairs. 'Bob's mother died about a year ago. It happened quite suddenly. A heart attack. His father was devastated, understandably. Well, he's in his late seventies and his own health isn't too good. I know Bob and Barbara hoped to persuade him to move here to live with them.' She frowned.

'Then, three months ago, Bob's father had a fall. Quite a bad one. He broke his hip. Bob and Barbara decided to move up there to be nearer to him, rather than try to uproot him. Instead of trying to sell this place, they decided to rent it out until they make more permanent plans.'

Neil grimaced wryly. 'It must have been a difficult time for them. I can't blame them for not wanting to give this up permanently.' He gazed round the room. 'I like it. I'd like to feel I was taking care of it for them in some small way.'

'As I said, it's quite large but I'm not sure how much space—how many rooms—you need.' Her gaze was drawn involuntarily to where he stood at the window, watching Jamie feed straw into the rabbit hutch. His back was to her, denying her any glimpse of his expression. 'Perhaps you'd like to discuss it first with your wife?'

'That won't be necessary. There's no one to discuss it with. I'm a widower.'

Beth stared at him. Her mouth suddenly felt dry. 'I. . .I'm so sorry. I had no idea.'

'It's all right.' He turned to look at her. 'There's no reason why you shouldn't know. My wife died four years ago when Jamie was just over a year old. She was involved in a road accident. Her car was hit by a lorry on the motorway. The driver had apparently fallen asleep at the wheel.'

Beth swallowed hard. 'I'm sorry,' she repeated. 'You must have been devastated.'

His mouth twisted. 'The irony was that Louise was on her way home from a keep-fit class. She was killed instantly. I suppose there was some comfort in that.'

'Was. . .was she a doctor?'

'A teacher.' There was an edge to his voice. 'She taught infants of Jamie's age. She loved her work. She was good at it.'

'I'm sorry. I can see why you feel you want to make a fresh start, but moving to somewhere so very differ-ent—isn't that rather drastic?'

He dug his hands in his pockets. 'If you mean, am I running away?' He frowned. 'I realised some time ago that I needed to move on, for Jamie's sake as much as my own. There were too many reminders, too many memories.'

Beth bit at her lip. 'Look, I'm sorry I stirred this up. I shouldn't have. . .'

'Don't be. I meant what I said. I'm sick of the rat race. I want more time for the important things. It's taken me a while, but I realise I've been working hard at the expense of the things that really matter. Besides. . .' his mouth twisted '. . .I may be wrong but I get the impression you haven't exactly been inundated with applicants.'

'Yes, well. . .' She flushed. 'I suppose Wadeley isn't everyone's cup of tea.'

'Oh, I don't know.' His mouth twisted. 'I'd say it has a lot going for it. Including the pubs.'

She swallowed hard. 'Look, I'm sorry about yes-terday.'

'Don't be.' He followed as she moved toward the door. 'I'm not going to have second thoughts, if that's what you're worried about. When I make a commitment I stick to it.' He held the door partially open, waiting for her to pass through. 'We got off to a bad start but we're both adults. I don't see any reason why we shouldn't be able to work together. Unless it's a prob-lem for you?'

She look up at him, disconcerted to find that they were suddenly very close. He smelled of expensive aftershave and danger, even though she couldn't, for the life of her, have explained why.

His blue eyes glinted, sending tiny ripples of shock running through her, and she swallowed hard.

'No, I don't see why it should be a problem.'

His gaze narrowed briefly as he seemed to study her, seeing the faint shadows beneath her eyes. 'Good,' he murmured, and for one incredible moment, as he bent his head and seemed to loom closer, she had the crazy feeling that he was going to kiss her.

She felt the breath catch in her throat as a feeling of physical awareness swept through her, then suddenly the kitchen door flew open and Jamie was standing there, looking at them quizzically.

'What are you doing?' He gazed from one to the other. 'Daddy, I like this house. It's nice and big, and it's got rabbits. I like Dr Maitland too. Can we come and live here, Daddy? Please?'

Neil released her immediately and, frowning, looked at his watch.

'We'll talk about it later, Jamie. Right now I think we'd better get Dr Maitland back to the surgery. I'd like to make it back to London before it gets dark. Oh, and before I forget. . .' He took a note from his pocket, pressing it into her nerveless hands. 'I think I owe you this.'

Without waiting for a response, he turned on his heel and walked away. But not before she had seen the cool amusement in his eyes.

She stared down at the crisp ten-pound note and felt the colour rising in her cheeks as she thrust it unceremoniously into her pocket.

Giving one last, hasty glance around, she snapped

the light off and locked the door, before making her way to the waiting car.

She didn't know anything about Neil Quinn except that he seemed to have the ability to provoke a great many conflicting emotions in her, none of which was going to make for an easy working relationship.

But, then, as he had said, they were both adults. There had to be a way of working things out—didn't there?

CHAPTER THREE

NINE days later winter seemed to have returned with a vengeance.

Beth locked her car door and hurried breathlessly into Reception, her cheeks flushed with cold as she headed through the busy waiting room and into the office.

Carefully sidestepping a lively youngster, she put her briefcase on the floor and blew on her fingers before she pocketed her keys and reached across the desk.

'Sorry I'm late. I had to de-ice the car. Are those for me?'

'Every last one.' Grinning, Emma handed over the stack of mail. 'Oh, and this is your list.'

Glancing at it, Beth groaned. 'Oh, great. I can see it's going to be one of those days. It's like Paddington station out there.'

'You'll be needing these.' Emma handed over a batch of cards, smiling as a young woman approached the desk. 'Morning, Mrs Bennett. Take a seat. Dr Quinn will be with you in a few minutes.'

Juggling her briefcase and the cards, Beth tried to push a wisp of hair from her eyes. 'He's here already?'

'Half an hour ago.' Emma grinned. 'And raring to go.'

Blast the man! Frowning, Beth hitched her bag more securely onto her shoulder. Wouldn't you just know it? His first day, the one day she was determined to get here on time, and her car had to play up.

'Give me a couple of minutes and you can wheel the

first patient in.' She had half turned away and was heading for the corridor when the bundle of cards began to slide from her grasp, cascading to the floor.

'Oh, no, that's all I need.' Annoyed by her own carelessness, she shifted her briefcase and bent to retrieve them—and collided heavily with another figure as it followed suit.

The breath was momentarily knocked out of her. She rocked backwards, flinging out an arm, and instinctively Neil reached out and drew her towards him as he steadied her.

'Here, you'd better let me.' In one easy movement he gathered up the cards, placing them in her hands.

Beth felt breathless. She was suddenly conscious of a crazy vortex of emotions that surged through her as she looked up at him.

'Thanks.' She pulled herself out of his grasp.

Blue eyes glinted. 'Aren't you just a little over-loaded?'

'No more than usual.' Colour flared in her cheeks. 'I was in a hurry. I meant to be here for your first morning, but I had trouble starting the car.'

'It was a nice thought, but you shouldn't have worried.'

She was beginning to wish she hadn't.

'That's not to say it isn't appreciated.' He gave a rueful smile, nodding briefly in the direction of the crowded waiting room. 'Is it always like this, or have I landed in the middle of some kind of epidemic?'

She laughed. 'It's more likely the curiosity factor.'

'Curiosity factor?' His dark brows drew together.

'Oh, some of them will be genuine enough, but I'd lay odds most of them have come along to give the new doctor the once-over.'

He grinned. 'In that case, let's hope I live up to their expectations.'

There wasn't likely to be much doubt about that, Beth thought. He was carrying his jacket slung over one shoulder, revealing tightly muscled arms and chest beneath a blue shirt. His casually styled black hair looked as if it had been recently trimmed.

She swallowed hard. Her own heart was beating just a shade too quickly, and she only had to work with the man!

She drew herself up sharply and glanced at her watch. 'Yes, well, I'd better get on or I'll still be here at teatime, judging from the look of things out there.' She paused. 'Look, I really am sorry you were dropped in at the deep end. I did mean to be here.'

'Forget it.'

Her mouth twisted. 'We wouldn't want to frighten you away before you've had a chance to find out what we're really like.'

'I told you, I don't quit that easily,' he said evenly. 'But, then, you don't know me very well yet, do you?'

A small pulse hammered at the base of her throat as she looked at him. 'Yes, well. . .' She cleared her throat. 'I must get on, but if you need any help don't be afraid to ask.'

She made her way to the consulting room, taking a few seconds to run a comb through her hair before pressing the bell to summon her first patient.

Her cheeks were still flushed from the cold wind, adding emphasis to her grey eyes. The thick mane of her hair was swept back, and she applied a touch of lipstick to her full, soft mouth. Her gaze travelled briefly over the jade polo-necked sweater and wide-belted full skirt. Moving to sit at the desk, she rang the bell and waited.

The time flew by, and it was almost a relief when her last patient of the morning came hesitantly into the consulting room. Beth looked up, smiling.

'Mrs Richards. Do make yourself comfortable and tell me what I can do for you.'

The woman toyed with her gloves, seeming uncertain where to begin. 'I went to the optician for a routine eye test.' She fingered her glasses nervously.

Beth waited for some further response and then, when none was forthcoming, swivelled her chair to withdraw the relevant notes from the folder. She glanced at them quickly, unfolding a recent letter. 'Ah, yes. You saw him just over a week ago.'

'That's right. The thing is. . .' Anna Richards frowned '. . .he did a test, with a sort of puffer thing.' She gave a nervous smile. 'It made me jump.'

Beth smiled. 'Yes, I know what you mean. It's quite painless. You just feel a tiny puff of air against your eye.'

The woman nodded. 'Well, he said my pressures were up a bit and he needed to do another test.' She frowned. 'I had to look into a machine and say when I saw flashing lights.'

'They call it a field test,' Beth explained. 'It's to test your field of vision.'

Anna Richards moistened her lips with her tongue. 'Well, he said he thought I might have glaucoma, and that he was going to write to you to arrange for me to see an eye specialist at the hospital in Shoremouth.'

Beth was already scanning the letter. 'Yes, I have it here.' She read it through quickly, then studied the woman. 'Are you worried about it?'

'Well—' Anna Richards broke off to stare fixedly at her hands again. 'The thing is, I don't know anything about glaucoma, you see.' Panic briefly widened her eyes. 'Does it mean I'm going blind?'

'No, absolutely not,' Beth was quick to reassure her. 'Admittedly, if it isn't diagnosed and treated early that *can* happen.'

'But surely I'd know if something was wrong?'

Beth shook her head. 'That's the problem. Glaucoma develops very slowly, over a period of years, and you probably wouldn't even know it was happening. That's why it's particularly important that people should have their eyes tested regularly so that any changes can be picked up. Glaucoma is a condition which affects the peripheral vision.'

Anna Richards looked at Beth. 'I have my eyes tested every two years, more or less. I knew my glasses needed changing.'

'That's fine,' Beth reassured her. 'The thing is that if it's caught early and treated the damage can be prevented.' She smiled. 'I promise you, there's nothing to worry about. The tests you'll have at the hospital are all quite simple and won't hurt a bit. You'll be asked to do a routine distance test, reading letters from a chart, just as you would at the opticians.'

'Well, I'm glad to hear that, anyway.'

Beth smiled. 'You'll have your blood pressure taken, and you'll probably be given another field test with more sophisticated equipment than the optician might have. After that, the consultant may put some drops in your eyes. Those are to dilate the pupils and help him to see much more clearly what's going on. He'll also shine a bright light into your eyes.'

Anna Richards looked at Beth. 'And that's it?'

'Yes.' Beth smiled. 'The consultant will have a chat with you and, depending on what the results of the tests are, he'll decide on a course of treatment.'

'I won't need an operation, will I?'

Beth shook her head. 'Glaucoma is usually treated with drops. If he decides you need them you may have to put them in every day. Even if you do have glaucoma it will have been caught in the early stages. You've been very sensible. You've had your eyes tested regularly so there's every reason to be optimistic.'

The older woman's anxious face was transformed by a smile. 'I feel so much better for having talked to you. I was so worried.'

'Yes, I can imagine.' Beth smiled sympathetically. 'I'll write to the hospital today, and you should get your appointment through fairly quickly.' As Anna Richards rose to her feet, heading for the door, Beth followed suit.

'I'm really grateful to you for taking the time to explain it to me.'

'No need. If you're at all worried, or need to talk, I'm here. Don't be afraid to come and see me any time.'

'I won't.'

Beth was on the point of closing her door when Neil appeared in the corridor that linked the consulting rooms. He was also seeing a patient out.

Beth felt the warm colour flood into her face as she felt the full weight of those blue eyes, studying her. 'Is everything all right?'

Neil gave a wry smile. 'I think I'll survive. I must have peered down at least ten throats this morning, and I'll swear not one of them was even remotely pink.'

'Lucky you. I could let you have Jack Taylor's ingrowing toenails, if you like. Or a nice case of haemorrhoids.'

'You're a real pal. Thanks but, no, thanks.'

'How are you settling in at the house?'

A smile twisted the corners of his mouth. 'It's just

as well it's furnished. At least we have beds to sleep in. Most of our stuff is still in boxes. I tell myself I'll make a concerted effort at the weekend to clear it.'

Beth frowned. 'What about Jamie? How's he taking the upheaval?'

'Oh, he thinks it's all great fun. But that's kids for you.'

'What happens while you're working? About Jamie, I mean?'

'Thanks to Alex, that's at least one problem I don't have to worry about. He suggested I talk to my neighbour, Sally Prentiss.'

'Oh, yes, I know Sally.' Beth frowned. 'Isn't she—?'

'A registered childminder? Answer to my prayers?' He grinned. 'I'd say so.' He glanced at his watch as the phone rang. 'Better not keep the patients waiting. I'll see you later maybe.'

Beth returned to her room to begin to clear her desk and try to organise her list of calls. She was doing a hasty recount of her patients' cards when a tap came at the door, just as she'd imagined she'd seen the last of the morning's patients.

Becky Dawson hovered uncertainly in the open doorway. 'Hi. Look, if this is a bad time just say. I don't have an appointment. . .'

'Becky!' Beth greeted her friend with a delighted grin. 'No, of course it's not a bad time. I've just finished, as a matter of fact. Come in. Oh, and you've brought the baby. Let me see.' She peered at the small bundle, enveloped in a shawl. 'Oh, Becky,' she breathed, brushing a finger gently against the velvety-soft skin. 'She's beautiful.'

The other girl grinned. 'Well, I happen to think so. I may be just ever so slightly biased, of course. Here, you hold her for a while. Give me a chance to get my breath back.'

Beth shook her head. 'No, you're not biased. It's not true, you know, that all babies are beautiful, but this one definitely is.' She took the tiny, sweet-smelling bundle into her arms, motioning her friend to a chair. 'How are you, anyway?'

'Me? Oh, I'm fine. A bit tired. I'm still getting used to the two o'clock feed lark. But George is very good.' She smiled. 'He offers moral support, even if he can't actually feed her himself.'

Beth gently unfolded the shawl, watching with delight as the baby stretched and yawned before a tiny fist found the small mouth and began sucking furiously. Gazing at the perfect little fingers and features, she felt her heart give an odd little lurch.

'I take it she enjoys her food?'

'She's a gannet. George keeps threatening to put her on a diet.'

Propping the baby against her shoulder, Beth grinned. 'He's obviously besotted.'

'We both are.' Becky sighed happily. 'Oh, Beth, she's absolutely the best thing that's happened to us. I wake up in the night sometimes and have to pinch myself to make sure it's really true. That's if she doesn't wake me first, of course.' She chuckled.

'Actually—' her gaze met Beth's '—that's the reason I came to see you. Apart from asking you to give her the once-over.' She smiled. 'George and I were wondering if you'd agree to be godmother?'

'Me! Oh, Becky, I'd be thrilled. If you're sure. . .?'

'Absolutely. You were number one on the list. Well, we've known each other long enough, haven't we? Since primary school.'

'Don't remind me.' Beth gave an exaggerated groan.

'It seems so long ago.' She settled the baby in the crook of her arm, smiling as one tiny fist grasped her finger. 'So, what have you decided to call her? We godparents need to know these things.'

'We finally decided on Hannah.'

'Hannah Dawson.' Beth tested the sound. 'It's lovely. *She's* lovely, aren't you, poppet?' She chuckled as the baby burped loudly.

'You've obviously got the magic touch.'

'Nice of you to say so, but I suspect touch had nothing to do with it. You'd been saving that one up, hadn't you, sweetheart? Come on, then, let's take a look at you. Not that I think you've anything remotely to worry about.' Gently she removed the shawl, resting the squirming baby on the examination couch as she looked at her friend. 'Anything you're worried about?'

'I thought she sounded a bit snuffly.'

'Hmm.' Almost automatically Beth checked the baby's limbs and hips, before reaching for her stethoscope. 'Well, she sounds fine. Babies do sometimes get snuffly. They can't cough or blow their noses. But, honestly, she seems fine. Come on, poppet. Back to Mum.' She handed over the baby who had begun to root for food. 'There's the store cupboard.'

'Tell me about it.' Groaning, Becky glanced at her watch. 'She's supposed to be on four-hourly feeds.'

Beth laughed. 'The trouble with babies is they can't tell the time.' Half sitting on the edge of the desk, she looked at her friend. 'Motherhood suits you.'

'Oh, I can recommend it. Apart from the fact that it plays havoc with the figure. You should try it, Beth.' Her fingers brushed the soft down on the baby's head. 'She's already made such a difference to our lives.' She kissed her daughter's velvety cheek.

'She's so special, Beth. I can't tell you how I feel.

I. . . I'd die for her. When I thought we might never have her, and George was so against the possibility of adoption—' She broke off, putting out a hand. 'Oh, Beth, I'm so sorry. I didn't mean. . .'

'Hey, it's all right.' Beth straightened her shoulders. 'Of course she's special.' She swallowed hard as a sudden and totally unexpected tremor ran through her. 'You know, it's ridiculous but I sometimes just wonder. . . Did *my* mother ever feel this way about me?'

Becky stared at her, her face anxious. 'Beth, I'm sure she did.'

Beth looked down at her friend's hand on her arm. 'It would have been nice to know for sure.' In a jerky movement she half turned away in an effort to battle the sudden surge of emotions that seemed to be welling up. 'Crazy, isn't it?' She gave a slight laugh. 'After all these years. I still think about her, wonder. . .what she was like. . .why. . .'

'That's only natural, Beth. But the Maitlands do love you, you know that?'

'Yes, of course they do. I've been lucky.' With an effort, she managed a smile. 'I'm just being silly. Adopting me was like an answer to their prayers, I know that. Next best thing to having a baby of their own.' She blew her nose hard and with a slight smile turned to her friend. 'They couldn't possibly have known that a couple of years later the real miracle would happen, could they?'

'You mean Michael.' Becky frowned.

Beth gave a slight laugh. 'Oh, you'd be surprised how often it happens. For no apparent reason a couple find they can't have children. After years of trying they decide to adopt and—hey presto—suddenly, perfectly naturally, the woman finds she's pregnant.' She swallowed hard, shocked by the depth of emotions she had imagined had long since been hidden. 'I really don't blame them,' she said huskily. 'I know how you and George felt about having a baby of your own—really of your own, I mean.'

Becky said quietly, 'I always thought you were happy with the Maitlands.'

Beth gave a ragged sigh as she raked a hand through her hair. 'I was. I'm sure they never *knowingly* treated us any differently. It wasn't their fault they loved Michael more.' She frowned. 'But I was aware of it. *I* knew that Michael was somehow more special.'

She straightened her shoulders, easing her muscles as she gazed fixedly at the sleeping baby. 'Anyway. . .' she laughed slightly '. . .aren't we getting just a little ahead of ourselves? There's one fairly important ingredient needed here. So far I haven't yet met the man I'd want to make that sort of commitment with.'

Becky looked at her. 'You know, I always thought that you and. . .' She frowned. 'What was his name?'

Beth's chin went up. 'James.'

'That's the one.' Becky eased the squirming baby against her shoulder. 'I always thought the two of you would make a go of it. Well, we all did, really. Of course, I didn't know him very well. But he seemed nice enough, and you seemed to get on so well together.'

Beth stifled a sigh and busied herself, tidying her desk. 'Yes, well, we did. But things didn't work out, that's all. You know how it is. It happens sometimes.'

A tiny frown tugged briefly at her brow. Despite the fact that it was more than three years since James had dropped his bombshell, by announcing that he had met someone else, it came as a shock to realise that she could still be hurt by what had happened—the suddenness of it all.

In one way she supposed she should be glad. After

all, it had provided the impetus she'd needed to finally take the plunge and leave the hospital and apply to join the Wadeley practice as a junior partner. Still suffering from delayed shock, she had felt she needed a complete break—a change of scene. Somewhere where she wouldn't have to see James and the new love of his life every day.

Looking back on it, the worst part of the whole nightmare had been the realisation that she had been the last to know what had been going on when it seemed that everyone else had known and been talking about it for months.

Sighing, she reflected that maybe she had only herself to blame. For as long as she could remember, she had dreamed of becoming a doctor. It had started around the age of seven when she had started bandaging her dolls and even the neighbours' cat.

The funny part was that she didn't even know where the idea had come from. It certainly hadn't been from her adoptive parents who, if they hadn't actively discouraged the idea, certainly hadn't encouraged it, urging her instead to learn to type—to get herself a good, solid job in an office.

But she had refused to be sidetracked. Training to become a doctor had been hard work and hadn't left much time for socialising, especially towards the end when her finals had been looming ever closer. Maybe that had been one of the reasons James had gradually become more and more disgruntled and had accused her of being a killjoy.

That had hurt. With his own finals safely behind him, she had expected if not sympathy then at least understanding. But James had clearly had other things on his mind.

She came back to reality with a start and the realis-

ation that the phone was ringing. Almost with a feeling
of relief, she reached for it. 'Yes?' She glanced at her
watch. 'Yes, I'll add him to my list of calls for this
morning. Thanks, Emma. Tell him I'll be with him in
about an hour, will you?'

Snow had turned to rain as half an hour later, having
hastily swallowed a cup of coffee, Beth ran out to her
car. Her first call was to Fillditch Farm. It was a routine
visit, and as she pulled up in front of the stone-built
farmhouse Carrie Simpson was on the step to greet her,
her weathered features beaming a welcome.

'Doctor, come in out of the cold.' Tall and wiry, she
led the way in. 'I've just brewed a pot of tea, if you'd
like a cup. There's a spot of home-made cake, too.'

'Carrie, I've been looking forward to it.' It was part
of the routine. Beth had soon learned that an important
part of general practice, especially in an area like
Wadeley, was getting to know her patients on a personal
basis and spending time with them. It was often the
best way of getting to hear about local problems, as
well as of winning people's trust. She had never viewed
this sort of socialising as a waste of time.

Seated at the table with a fire crackling in the hearth
and a mug of strong tea and a wedge of cake in front
of her, Beth looked at the older woman.

'So, how are things, then, Carrie? It must be about
three weeks since I last popped over to see you.'

'Aye, something like that.' Carrie Simpson was fifty
years old but looked more as she glanced at the man
seated in a chair by the fire. 'Dad's pretty much the
same. Well, you can see for yourself. I have to keep
an eye on him all the time in case he takes it into his
head to wander off. Some days he seems a bit better
than others.'

Beth nodded sympathetically. Harry Simpson was

seventy-five years old and had been diagnosed two years ago as having Alzheimer's disease. His condition had deteriorated noticeably in the past six months so that, without help, he was no longer able to carry out even the simplest of tasks—such as dressing and feeding himself—without help.

Leaving her tea, Beth went to sit beside the man and took his frail hand in her own. 'Hello, Harry. It's Dr Maitland. Do you remember me? I've just popped in to have a chat to Carrie, and to see how you are.'

Harry Simpson gazed at her, seeming to study her features, before he returned his gaze to the crackling fire.

'You'll not get any sense out of him,' Carrie said, with brisk resignation. 'He'll forget a conversation we had two minutes ago.'

'Yes, I'm afraid that's one of the classic symptoms of the disease. It must be very distressing for you.' Beth gently squeezed Harry Simpson's hand as she straightened up. 'How does he seem, otherwise?'

'He's been a bit chesty this past couple of days.'

'Well, at least I can check him over for you.' Reaching for her stethoscope, Beth spoke reassuringly to the man as she listened to his chest.

'I don't think there's anything serious to worry about,' she said as she straightened up moments later. 'It doesn't sound as if there's any infection there. I'll leave you a prescription for some linctus, which should help. But if you're at all worried give me a call at the surgery.'

'Aye, I'll do that.' Carrie settled a rug over her father's legs. 'Best finish your tea while it's hot, Dad.'

Beth sipped at her own cup. 'It's you I'm really worried about, Carrie,' she said gently. 'Nursing someone, especially someone close to you, who has

Alzheimer's is an exhausting and sometimes soul-destroying job, no matter how much you might love them.'

For a few seconds Carrie Simpsons's eyes were sus-piciously bright. She blinked hard. She had been brought up on the farm which had, until a few years ago, been run by her father. She had been an only child and had grown up tough, knowing that she was depended upon to give a hand.

Rumours had it that there had been one serious love in Carrie's life. It hadn't survived her parents' need of her and she hadn't looked at a man since. At least, not with marriage in mind.

Gradually, after her mother's death and her father's obviously deteriorating health, Carrie had taken over the running of the farm. The results were painfully obvious, but Carrie Simpson had never been a quitter and she wasn't about to start now.

She swallowed hard. 'Aye, it's not easy, seeing one of your own reduced to summat no better than a veg-etable. He doesn't even know who I am now, and that's hard.'

Beth bit at her lower lip. 'We could get you some help, Carrie. There are places—'

'No.' Carrie reached decisively for the teapot as she rose to her feet. 'I know you mean well, Doctor, and don't think it's not appreciated. But I can look after my own, thank you very much. He's my dad and I'll look after him as long as I can. He'd want that.'

Beth smiled gently, pushed back her chair and looked at Carrie's pale, drawn features, realising she wasn't getting anywhere. 'Well, you know where I am, Carrie. If ever you decide you do need extra help, or just moral support. . .'

'I'll keep your number by me, Doctor.'

Beth held back a sigh as she gathered up her bag and coat. 'I'll call in again, Carrie.'

'Aye.' The woman held open the door. 'You're always welcome any time, Doctor.'

As Beth made her way to the car she heard the plaintive cry of Harry Simpson, demanding attention once again. Inserting the key into the lock she glanced back at the house, but Carrie had already gone and the door was closed.

Beth headed back along the coast road, catching an occasional glimpse of the pewter-coloured sea in the bay below.

It was another two hours and almost dark by the time she had made the last of her calls and was finally able to head for home.

The faint glimmering of the late afternoon sun had long since gone, and the air already struck with a deepening chill, heralding a frost.

Stifling a yawn, she turned the car down the hill to the narrow lane where a distant gleam of light from the Scotts' old house came into view, and she realised that Neil would have finished afternoon surgery over an hour ago.

She followed the road down to the harbour, bringing the car to a halt in front of a terrace of what had once been a row of fishermen's cottages. As she climbed out and locked the car door the faint smell of cooking drifted appetisingly to her nostrils. Letting herself in, she was met by a large, ginger cat who came, purring noisily, to brush against her legs.

'Henry.' She bent to fondle his ears. 'So, what sort of day have you had, then?' As if she needed to ask. The collapsed state of his favourite cushion was ample evidence that he probably hadn't even moved from his basket. 'You lazy old thing. And now I suppose you want feeding?'

Automatically, as she opened a tin of cat food, she glanced at the bundle of mail she had collected from the mat on her way in. 'Two bills, one circular. Yes, well, they can wait. There you go, then.' She set the dish on the floor. 'Your favourite, pilchards and prawn, and don't say I never do anything for you.'

She shed her jacket and removed from the oven the casserole she had thrown together that morning, before leaving for work. Lifting the lid, she gazed with dismay at the contents.

'I must have had a brainstorm. There's enough here to feed a small army.' Or certainly enough for two extra people—a tiny inner voice took a swipe at her conscience. A mental image of Neil Quinn and his small son, surrounded by a mountain of packing cases, swam before her eyes, only to be brushed aside as swiftly as it arose.

She glanced hopefully at the cat, then shook her head. 'No, perhaps not.' She raked a hand through her hair. 'Dammit, Henry, Neil Quinn is a grown man and more than capable of taking care of himself,' she declared roundly.

Henry dragged his head from his empty dish to give her a baleful stare, before swishing his tail and stalking away.

'Fat lot of use you are.' She stared at the steaming dish, sighed heavily and reached for her jacket and the car keys.

A faint sound of classical music came from somewhere within the house as she stood on Neil's doorstep, her hand hovering over the bell.

He's probably sitting in front of the fire with his feet

up, watching television, and I'm going to look like an idiot, she thought. Oh, come on, she told herself decisively. It's just a friendly gesture—hand over the casserole and leave. Simple.

Her hand jabbed at the bell and she turned to gaze at the distant darkened fields. The night sky was clear, a sure sign of frost, and her breath fanned white into the air as she waited.

'Well, this is a nice surprise.' The quiet drawl came from behind her. 'Now, don't tell me, let me guess. You're the Avon lady?'

She spun round, almost dropping the dish in the process, and felt herself flush as her gaze drifted upwards to meet the glint of mischief in Neil Quinn's eyes.

'Actually, I brought you this. I'm afraid it's only chicken casserole. . .'

'Only!' The blue eyes glinted.

She swallowed hard. 'I made too much, and it occurred to me that you probably hadn't had time to shop and might be able to use it.' She could hear herself babbling.

His hair was wet, as if he had just showered, and the faint smell of aftershave drifted into her nostrils. He was dressed in jeans, the material stretched tautly against the hard muscles of his thighs. Neil Quinn looked powerfully masculine.

'Of course, you've probably already eaten. . .'

He gave a slight chuckle as he drew his hand from behind his back to reveal a tin opener. 'I was just about to throw some beans into a saucepan. But I have to say that faced with this kind of temptation. . .' He stretched out a muscular arm. She stiffened, feeling the breath catch in her throat, then the colour flared defensively in her cheeks again as he lifted the lid and inhaled deeply.

'Beans on toast is a non-starter. Look, why don't you come in? We're not exactly straight yet, but we're getting there slowly.'

'Oh, no, really. I didn't mean to intrude.' She had already half turned away.

'You won't be intruding,' he said evenly. 'Look, have you eaten yet?'

'Well, no.' She hesitated.

'In that case, why not join us?' He grinned, indicating the dish. 'You said yourself there's more than enough for two. Besides, I'm sure Jamie would like to see you again, and I'd rather like to talk to you.'

She flicked a glance in the direction of the cool blue gaze, and wished she hadn't as her eyes encountered his mouth, firm and attractive and, illogically, far too much of a threat to her peace of mind.

With an effort she hauled back her wayward thoughts. What was she thinking of? She didn't even know this man.

'It is rather late.'

His mouth quirked. 'It's business, Beth. There's a patient I need to discuss. I'm worried about her.'

She moistened her lips with the tip of her tongue. 'Well, in that case. . .'

Somehow, without her even being quite sure how it had happened, he had taken her coat and led her into the sitting room. 'Make yourself at home. I'll just pop this into the oven to keep it hot.'

She stood uncertainly, and looked around her. Already he had begun to make changes. There were new curtains and cushions, and pictures on the walls. She wondered what he would do to the rest of the house. The bedrooms. . .

'Jamie, look who's come to see us. It's nice Dr Maitland. Come and say hello.'

She turned as the door opened and Jamie, his face covered in a multitude of brightly coloured face paints, came into the room.

'Well, hello again.' She smiled. 'I can see you've been busy.'

'I'm a pirate.'

'So I see, and a very handsome one at that.'

Neil looked up, his gaze locking intently with hers for a few seconds. She swallowed convulsively, feeling suddenly like an intruder. Smiling slightly, she bent down so that she was on a level with the small boy. 'That sword looks very dangerous.' She gave a mock shiver.

Jamie leaned against the chair, one leg crossed over the other as he brandished the weapon. 'It isn't a sword.' He fixed her with a disdainful look. 'It's a cuckliss.'

Neil made a slight sound in his throat and Beth felt her own lips twitch. Reaching into her pocket, she produced a tube of the colourful, chocolate-filled sweets she always kept handy for when she might be visiting a smaller patient.

'Would you like a sweet?'

Jamie considered her gravely, glancing at his father before resting his head against the arm of the chair. 'No, fank you.'

Her gaze flew up to meet Neil's. 'Oh, look, I'm sorry. I shouldn't have asked.'

'It's all right.' He smiled ruefully. 'Our neighbour. . .'

'The childminder?'

He nodded. 'Sally has twin boys. They're about six months older than Jamie. It's their birthday today. They had a bit of a party and someone ate a bit too much.' His mouth quirked. 'We're feeling a bit sorry for ourselves.' He ruffled his son's hair. 'Believe it or not, he scrubs up quite well.'

'Daddy!' A small hand tugged at his jeans. 'I feel sick.'

'I think I'd better go and sort things out.' Neil looked at her as he swept his son up into his arms. 'I won't be long. Make yourself at home. Help yourself to a drink or coffee. I'll be down in a few minutes.'

She glanced uneasily at him. 'Look, wouldn't it be best if—?'

'I really would like to talk to you, if you can spare the time.'

She stifled a sigh and nodded, watching as he disappeared with his son before making her way slowly to the kitchen.

She made coffee and carried it to the kitchen table, where she kicked off her shoes and sat, looking around her. There were subtle changes here too. Again, there were new curtains. She could see pairs of wellingtons— one large, the other small, bright, shiny blue—standing side by side on a small mat. It was a warm room, cosy, disorganised as yet but already a home.

There was something vaguely unsettling about being here and sharing, even vicariously, the intimacy of Neil's home.

A slight sound made her start and she looked up to see Neil, standing in the doorway. He was studying her so intently that she put down her cup quickly, spilling some of her coffee in the saucer.

'I'm sorry, I'm afraid I started without you.'

'Good.' he reached for his own cup. 'I'm sorry about that.'

'How is he?'

'Asleep. He didn't even ask for his favourite bedtime story.'

She pulled a face. 'As serious as that?'

'Absolutely.' His slow smile did things to her already overworked pulse rate.

She pushed her cup away. 'You have a lovely little boy.'

'I think so.'

'I suppose Jamie inherited that gorgeous fair hair from his mother.'

His expression was unreadable. 'Yes, Jamie takes after his mother in looks. His temperament, I'm afraid, is all mine. He tends to know what he wants and usually manages to get it.'

She could believe it. 'You must miss his mother very much.'

A spasm flickered briefly across his features. 'My biggest regret is that Louise missed out on seeing Jamie grow up, just as Jamie has missed out on not having her around when he most needs her.'

'If it's any consolation,' she said softly, 'I think you've done a great job.'

He looked at her. 'I'm flattered, but it's hardly the same, is it?'

He still loves her, she thought, and was shocked to experience a feeling which she absolutely refused to acknowledge as jealousy.

'You're doing your best, Neil. Anyone can see that.'

His mouth twisted. 'I'm just not always sure it's good enough.' He drained his cup and rose to his feet. 'I thought we could eat and talk at the same time, if that's all right with you.'

She stared at him, then blinked hard as she felt the faint colour stir in her cheeks. 'Yes, of course. That will be fine.'

He placed the casserole dish on the table and, as if by magic, produced a dish of rice from the microwave.

'Not very imaginative, I'm afraid,' he said with a grin, 'but it sure beats baked beans.'

Beth hadn't imagined she would be hungry, but when it came to it she was found she was—ravenous, in fact. Confronted by the richness of the casserole and crusty bread—accompanied by what she guessed was a superb red wine—she ate enthusiastically.

In no time at all, it seemed, her plate was empty and she sat back, disconcerted to find him watching her with a gleam of amusement in his eyes.

'I must have been more hungry than I thought,' she confessed, slightly shamefacedly.

Neil chuckled. 'Don't apologise. After five years of feeding Jamie, who despises anything other than beans and fish fingers, it's a pleasure to see someone enjoy their food.' He raised a glass. 'My compliments to the chef. We must do this again some time,' he said softly. 'On the understanding, of course, that next time I provide the food.'

She gulped at her red wine, coughed and said, 'So, what did you want to talk about? You said something about a patient?'

'That's right. Her name is Wheeler. Grace Wheeler. She came to see me yesterday. I'm rather hoping you'll know something about her background.'

'Wheeler?' Frowning, she shook her head. 'Doesn't ring any bells. Grace Wheeler... Oh, wait, yes, there is something. Mid-thirties? One of Bob's patients?'

'That's the one.'

She frowned. 'Now that you mention it, I think I did see her. Bob was on leave at the time. What's the problem?'

'I'm not entirely sure that there is a problem. You could call it more of a gut feeling. I thought if you knew something about the background it might give me a clearer picture into what's going on.'

He rose to his feet, brought the coffee-pot to the table and filled their cups. 'She wanted a repeat prescription for antidepressant tablets.'

'If it's a repeat prescription presumably Bob had prescribed them?'

He nodded. 'According to her notes, they were first prescribed a few months ago and he'd been seeing her on a regular basis.'

'That sounds like normal procedure.'

'I agree.' He stirred sugar into his coffee. 'What I'm not too clear on is the background. I gather there was some sort of domestic trouble—marriage problems, something like that.'

'I don't know all the details, and I suppose Bob would only know what she told him. But, yes, I think her husband left her.' Beth frowned.

'I seem to remember it was all pretty tragic. I do know that Mrs Wheeler suffered a stillbirth. There aren't any other children. She took it pretty badly, naturally enough. Bob prescribed antidepressants and then, some time ago, I heard—just rumours—that her husband had walked out. But I don't know any of the details.' She looked at Neil. 'Does it help?'

'I think so.' He took their empty cups and a dish to the sink, leaning against it as he turned to look at her. 'I'm not happy about prescribing any antidepressant or tranquilliser over a long period of time.' He frowned.

'I'm not saying they don't have their uses. But we both know that patients can become dependent or, after a while, the medication itself can produce adverse effects. Sleeplessness.' He gave a slight laugh. 'Even anxiety states.'

'I agree.' She frowned as she rose to her feet, clearing

wine glasses and handing him another dish. 'But if Grace Wheeler isn't coping, and clearly she isn't. . .'

'I'm not suggesting an instant withdrawal of the tablets.' He raked a hand through his hair. 'That would be irresponsible and counter-productive. She needs to be weaned off them gradually. But I do feel that she might benefit from some counselling. There's a national support group for women who've gone through the trauma of stillbirth.'

'I take it you've already suggested it?'

Neil nodded.

'And how did she take it?'

'Hard to tell. She was used to Bob Scott. I'm still very much the new boy, still on trial. Right now I suspect she, and a few others, thinks I'm not the most sympathetic person on earth.'

She grinned. 'Poor you. Mr Unpopularity. Still, don't let it get to you. I'm sure you'll win them round—eventually.'

'I'm not actually looking for a vote of confidence, though that would be nice.' His mouth curved. 'It's always easier to work with people who are friends. Don't you find that?'

Strangely flustered, Beth moved away to collect the rest of the dishes. 'If it's any consolation I think you did the right thing. But, then, you don't need my approval.'

'All the same,' he said evenly, removing the dishes from her grasp and setting them aside, 'it's good to have it.'

'The Maitland seal of approval.' She laughed, then drew away shakily as his gaze seemed to narrow briefly, roaming over the soft tumble of her hair to the slight flush in her cheeks.

His dark brows drew together. 'By the way, I haven't

thanked you for tonight—for the food, for the company. The advice. I'm really very grateful.'

She gave a slightly breathless laugh. 'There's no need—'

'I think there is.' He frowned. 'You didn't have to do any of it. I just want you to know that it's appreciated, that's all.'

She felt the colour surge into her cheeks, suddenly conscious of a crazy vortex of emotions that surged through her like a tidal wave as she forced herself to look up at him. 'Didn't they tell you? It's what partners are for.'

He gave a slight smile. 'I'd like to think we can be friends as well as partners. Don't you think we could at least give it a try?'

Friends! Somehow she felt it wasn't a word she would ever be able to apply to her feelings about Neil Quinn. She drew a deep breath. How did you deal with an unknown quantity?

Almost as if he'd read her thoughts, he frowned and said softly, 'Is it really so difficult?'

Right now she was finding it difficult to concentrate on anything, except the very strange effect his nearness was having on her nervous system. Her gaze was drawn to the sensuous mouth and the dark eyes which seemed to be drawing her out of her depth.

She heard his slight intake of breath, saw him frown and was totally unprepared for his touch as slowly his thumb lightly grazed the sweet fullness of her mouth. 'Friends, Beth. That's all I'm asking.'

She stood, mesmerised by the power of the sensations that coursed through her, and her breath caught in her throat as a new realisation came homing in to her bemused senses. If she wasn't very careful there was

every danger of her becoming seriously attracted to
Neil Quinn.

A tremor ran through her. 'It's getting late.' She was
breathing raggedly as she moved away. 'I really should
be going.' Her voice sounded oddly husky.

'I'll see you in the morning.'

She nodded and reached for her jacket, rejecting his
help when he would have helped her into it. He followed her to the door.

'Will you be all right?'

'Fine.' She would be once her heart had steadied to
its normal rate.

He came out with her as she unlocked the car door,
their breath streaming white into the freezing night air.

'I hope Jamie will soon be better.'

His mouth quirked as he held the door open while
she climbed in. 'Kids are amazing. He'll sleep it off
and be right as rain by morning.'

Lucky Jamie, she thought. 'I'm sorry I didn't really
get a chance to chat to him.'

'Never mind.' His mouth twisted. 'There'll be plenty
more opportunities.'

His sudden, slow smile did things to her already
overworked pulse rate. Then she realised that he was
still holding the door open.

'I'll see you in the morning, then,' he said softly as
he closed it.

She nodded, then eased the car down the drive and
onto the road.

Neil Quinn might to all intents and purposes, have
been free, but the truth was that he was still committed,
she realised. He still loved his wife and he had a small
son who must be a constant, daily reminder of her. It
didn't seem likely that he would want to get involved
again—did it?

CHAPTER FOUR

'OH, WONDERFUL, that's all I need.' Beth drew the curtains and pulled a face at the rain lashing the kitchen windows.

Swallowing the dregs of her now-cold cup of coffee, she gave a small wail of protest as she glanced at the clock. It was definitely going to be one of those mornings. She had somehow managed to sleep right through the alarm, and the toaster had jammed, nearly cremating the only remaining slice of bread. And now the heavens had opened.

She shrugged herself into her coat and grabbed her bag and her keys, before realising that Henry was parading none too happily before the door.

'What?' she demanded crossly. 'I don't have time for this, Henry. You can't want to go out again. No cat in his right senses would want to go out in this. Only crazy humans do that sort of thing.' And I'm going to be late if I don't get a move on, she thought' and sighed heavily as, tail swishing, Henry overruled her, glaring pointedly at the door until, finally, she succumbed.

'Right. On your own head be it.' She shivered as the open door let in a flurry of rain and freezing cold air. 'Some cats would appreciate a nice warm basket and the run of the house, but who am I to argue?'

Henry was gone for ages. Another glance at the clock sent her heading for the door. Hesitating briefly, she looked out at the torrent of rain, pulled up her collar and made a dash for the car.

She had left it parked in the open and the yard was

slippery with damp and leaves. As she hurried towards it, keys at the ready, her foot suddenly seemed to skid out from under her and she gave a sharp cry of pain as her heel tipped sideways, wrenching her ankle and sending a shock wave of pain running through her.

For a few seconds she felt physically sick as she closed her eyes and clung on, waiting for the pain to subside.

'This is definitely my lucky day,' she muttered through gritted teeth, wincing as gingerly she tried testing her weight on the injured foot. It was several seconds before she finally managed to climb in behind the wheel, already resigned to arriving late at the surgery.

One look at the packed car park told her they were in for a busy morning. She locked the car and made her way through to Reception, wincing as every step gave a painful reminder of her rapidly swelling ankle.

'Hi, sorry I'm late. I don't suppose you have a couple of aspirin handy?'

Emma grinned as she added another card to the growing pile. 'Been at the red wine, have we?' Her face sobered as she looked at Beth's pale features. 'You look awful.'

'Thanks a lot.' Beth managed a faint smile. 'I twisted my ankle, and the red wine had nothing to do with it. It's still a bit painful, that's all.'

'Oh, lor. Well, look, Annie's in the treatment room. Her first patient hasn't arrived yet. Do you want me to get her to take a look at it for you?'

Glancing at the rapidly filling waiting room, Beth shook her head. 'I think I'd better make a start or we'll have a mutiny on our hands.' Easing the weight off her injured foot, she performed a balancing act as she gathered her bag and a rapidly growing bundle of cards.

'If I have time, and if she's still around, I'll probably pop in to see her later.'

Emma looked doubtful. 'I really think you should get it seen to. You could have a fracture.'

'I don't think so.' Even though it was hurting more by the minute. 'If it gets any worse I may get an X-ray, but right now I'd—'

'Problems?' The quiet drawl came from behind her.

Without thinking, she turned sharply, and gasped as the pain in her ankle surged again. Instinctively she bit at her lower lip. Her glance flickered over Neil's dark trousers, pale blue shirt and the bronzed column of his throat. Warm colour suffused her cheeks as she closed her eyes for a brief moment, shutting out the image. He was far too attractive for her peace of mind.

'Beth's twisted her ankle,' Emma announced, blithely ignoring her small sigh of frustration. 'I was just saying she should get it checked.'

Neil was instantly concerned. 'Emma's right. You'd better let me take a look.'

'It's nothing, really. A bit of a sprain, that's all. It'll be fine.' She swallowed hard.

Neil gazed at her already swollen ankle and frowned. 'Emma's right. It needs looking at—*now*. It won't take more than a few minutes. It probably just needs a firm strapping, but it would be a lot less painful. Why not let me take a look?'

His own gaze lingered on the calf-length full skirt she had elected to wear. She had teamed it with a tan-coloured polo-neck sweater, opting for practicality, warmth and neatness rather than fashion.

'I'm sure you're right.' Restively, she tucked a stray tendril of hair behind her ear. 'I'll see to it later when I don't have a waiting room full of patients.' She should have known it wouldn't be that easy as Neil's mouth took on an ominously stubborn look.

'There are two ways we can do this, Beth. You can walk or I can carry you. Which is it to be?' His blue eyes glinted and she felt the breath catch in her throat as a feeling of physical awareness swept through her.

She glared at him, biting back what she knew would be a futile protest.

'Hold onto me. I'll help you through to my room.'

'There's really no need for this.'

'Let me be the judge of that.' She became conscious of the warm, masculine strength of him as he supported her, one arm round her waist. 'Just sit there and let's take a look.'

He sat opposite her and reached down to take her ankle in his hands. He began to flex it gently, moving it carefully from one side to the other. The cool touch of his hands on her flesh was utterly unexpected and startlingly intimate as his fingers brushed against her skin.

Surprise brought warm colour into her cheeks, but once the initial moment had passed there was no denying that it was a disconcertingly pleasurable experience, Beth thought as she closed her eyes and, wincing, opened them again suddenly to encounter the familiar dark shape of his head only inches away.

'Is that painful?'

Biting at her lip, she nodded.

'I thought so.' He straightened. 'Well, if it's any consolation, I'm pretty sure it's a sprain. I'll put a support strapping on it for you. Even so, I'm afraid it's probably going to be pretty painful for a while. I can let you have some tablets, if you like. But if it doesn't seem to be getting any better in a few days I want you to get it checked again. Either I can do it or you can see Annie. Is that understood?'

She flashed him a look. 'You're a bully, Dr Quinn. I suppose you know that?'

A nerve pulsed in his jaw. 'So I've been told. I think I can live with it.'

Blue eyes met hers and she swallowed hard. Her nostrils filled with the warm, male scent of him, teasing her senses and filling her with confusion. She felt dazed by her reaction to a man she scarcely knew—wasn't even sure she wanted to know.

They stared into each other's eyes. 'I. . .er.' She cleared her throat. 'How's Jamie?'

'Fine.' His mouth curved. 'I dare say he won't want to see another ice cream in a hurry but, otherwise, he's back to normal.'

'I'm glad.' She found herself gazing with fascination at his hair, which curled slightly against his collar, before her gaze rose to meet the full impact of his blue eyes.

'Sleep well?' he asked.

'Like a log, thanks.' She crossed her fingers mentally on the lie.

'I'm glad.' He frowned as he seemed to study her in silence for several moments, his eyes narrowing on the shadows beneath her eyes. She saw him tense briefly and was totally unprepared as, very slowly, he bent his head and the sensuous mouth moved closer, then his lips brushed against hers.

It was the sheer unexpectedness of it that caught her off guard. Or, at least, that was what she told herself. For a moment she resisted, but it *was* only a moment before she found herself swaying towards him, moaning softly and surrendering to an overwhelming need as her body betrayed her with its instant response. There was something to be said for will-power, but right now she couldn't think what it was.

For an instant she felt him tense, then she was free, his breathing harsh as he drew away. Confused, she looked up, a protest beginning to form, then she became dizzyingly aware of the open door.

'Ah, Neil, glad I caught you.' The voice of Annie Collins, the practice nurse, broke into the tension.

Only then, as the warm tide of colour washed into her cheeks, was Beth aware of Neil deliberately shielding her from the other girl's gaze, gaining her the precious seconds she needed to recover.

She raked a hand through her hair, only too aware of how she must look. Her cheeks were flushed and the button of her skirt had somehow managed to come undone.

'Not caught you at a bad moment, have I?' Annie hovered in the doorway. 'Only I was hoping you'd sign a couple of prescriptions for me before I start on Mr Murray's dressing.'

'Not at all. I think we've solved the problem, don't you, Dr Maitland?' The faint gleam in Neil's eyes wasn't lost on Beth. 'The strapping should do the trick.' He turned to her. 'I'll let you have those tablets. If you feel at all worried. . .'

Beth choked. 'I'll be sure to take them, thank you.'

A spasm flickered across his features as she straightened her shoulders, purposely avoiding his gaze. 'Yes, well, if you'll excuse me.'

Minutes later, scanning her notes, she popped her head round the door of the waiting room, to be confronted by a sea of hopeful faces.

'Mr Martin, sorry I'm late starting. Would you like to come through now, please? Make yourself comfortable. . .' she indicated the chair '. . .and tell me what I can do for you.'

She knew David Martin quite well. He was forty years old, a teacher and a keep-fit fanatic, so it came as something of a surprise to see him sitting opposite her, looking pale and less than happy.

'I think I'm going deaf,' he said, without preamble. 'I've got this ringing noise in my ear.' He held his hand up to the right side of his head. 'Everything sounds muffled. I noticed it in class a few days ago.' He gave a slight smile. 'I thought everyone had suddenly started talking in whispers. You know, just to wind me up. Then gradually I realised it was me.'

'Have you had any earache—pain in the ear?' Beth was on her feet, reaching for her auroscope.

'Well, it was bothering me a bit last week. I got this sudden stabbing pain and it's been giving me trouble ever since.'

'Let's take a look and see if we can see what's going on.' She made her examination, checking both ears as gently as possible. Even so, Dave Martin flinched. 'Sorry about that.' She straightened. 'Well, I'm not surprised it's painful or that you can't hear properly. The right ear looks quite nasty.'

Seating herself at the desk again, she brought up the patient's previous history on the computer screen. 'Have you noticed any bleeding or discharge from the ear?'

'Well, yes, on both counts.'

'Any dizziness?'

He pulled a face.

'Dave, why didn't you come and see me before this?'

'Probably a case of burying my head in the sand.' He looked slightly sheepish. 'My dad went deaf. It happened gradually so I suppose we didn't notice it too much.' He looked at her. 'I panicked a bit, thought history was repeating itself. I could see the job and everything else going down the drain.'

Beth gave an exasperated smile. 'I'd say panic is the word. What you've got is a ruptured eardrum. have you been poking at your ear with a stick or cotton-wool swab or anything?'

'Hardly.'

'Oh, believe me, you'd be surprised what people stick in their ears.' She smiled. 'I suppose Janet hasn't kissed you over the ear?'

He grinned. 'Not that I particularly remember.'

'No, well, I have to rule out every possibility.'

'And you're saying a kiss can do it?'

'It can if it's done with sufficient pressure.' She smiled. 'Seriously, I think what's happened is that you've picked up a middle-ear infection and that's caused the rupture.'

'Is it going to mean an operation?' Dave Martin asked anxiously as she keyed the information into the computer.

'Hopefully not. I'll give you some antibiotics to clear the infection. If the eardrum doesn't become infected it will usually repair itself within about two months.'

'And if it does become infected?'

'I think you're being unnecessarily pessimistic but, all right, if it does it's curable with treatment, and hearing is not usually affected permanently.'

Dave Martin breathed a sigh of relief. 'So I'm not ready for the scrap heap yet?'

'Sorry,' She grinned. 'You've got at least another twenty years or so, I'm afraid.' She handed him a prescription. 'Take these as directed and *finish the course*. You can take something like paracetamol if you feel you need something for the pain.' She rose to her feet and Dave Martin followed suit.

'Don't blow your nose too hard, and no swimming. Try putting a small wad of cotton wool in your ear when you bathe or shower to keep the moisture out.'

'Will do.' He headed happily for the door.

'And come back and see me again if the pain persists or you think it's getting worse.'

With a wave of his hand he went on his way, and Beth returned to her desk. It was a busy morning, during which she saw a steady stream of patients. There was the inevitable spate of coughs and sore throats, most of which she felt would have been better treated simply by the patients staying at home and taking whatever form of cold relief suited them best. Though there were a few, particularly the very young or the elderly, who did require antibiotics.

Several pensioners took advantage of the fact that it was market day to combine a shopping trip with a visit to the surgery in order receive an annual flu jab. She confirmed a pregnancy, referred a suspected diabetic to the appropriate consultant and diagnosed an advanced case of measles in a fretful three-year-old.

All in all, it had been a hectic morning. Her ankle was throbbing and she was looking forward to her afternoon off and a long, peaceful soak in a hot bath.

Gathering her coat and briefcase, she was on her way through to Reception just as Neil came out of his own consulting room. Studiously avoiding his gaze, she leaned across the desk, where Ruth Baxter was answering the telephone, to hand the cards to Emma.

'There are a couple of letters,' she prompted. 'If you wouldn't mind doing them today? I'd like to get Mr Phillips's referral to the haematologist through as quickly as possible.'

'Right, leave it with me. I'll see to it.' Emma scanned the notes and smiled.

Beth was almost at the door when Ruth called her, her voice anxious as she replaced the phone.

'Beth, I've just had a call from May Rawlings, up at Chalk Ridge Farm. She sounds in quite a panic. She was asking for Alex. I've explained that he's away on a course—'

'That's all right. I'll take it.' Beth hobbled back to the desk. 'What's the problem?'

'The tractor's overturned. She says Jim is trapped and he's hurt. She's tried to move him but she's afraid of doing more damage.'

Beth felt her heart skip a beat. 'Has she called for an ambulance?'

'Yes, but it's been snowing quite heavily and it's settled. There's no telling how long it might be before it gets there.'

Frowning, Beth looked at her watch and then out of the window, where a leaden grey sky gave evidence of rapidly plummeting temperatures. 'He'll freeze to death out there.'

'I'll take the call.' Neil spoke evenly from behind her.

She turned to look at him, her mind already assessing the time it would take to get to the injured man and what she would find when she got there.

She shook her head. 'I know Jim Rawlings. I have to go. May would want me to be there.'

'Then I'm coming with you.' His voice brooked no argument, and she felt a tiny surge of relief run through her. 'I'll be with you in a few seconds. Just let me get my bag. We can take my car.'

Mercifully, the narrow roads up to the farm were still relatively clear of snow. When they got there May

Rawlings was waiting in the yard, her face stiff and pale with cold and anxiety.

'Where is he, Mary?'

'Up in the top field.' Hugging her coat around her, she was already leading the way, her head lowered against the biting wind.

'Can you tell me what happened?'

'I don't know for sure. He was taking some feed and bales of straw up to the top pasture. It was young Jason, the lad who comes in to help with the milking, who noticed Jim wasn't back.' May Rawlings's distraught face crumpled. 'He found Jim pinned under the tractor.'

'Was he conscious?' Neil asked grimly, matching his longer strides to their own, his hand beneath May's elbow.

She shook her head. 'He said not. Jason's a bright lad. He managed to reach Jim's mobile phone. He called me. I went up there to see—' Her voice broke. 'He looks awful. So pale, and there was blood. . .'

'But he was breathing?'

She nodded, brushing a hand shakily against her lips. 'I rang for the ambulance and the fire brigade. They're going to have to lift the tractor to get him out. Then I rang the surgery.' She motioned towards the surrounding snow-covered hills.

'With this drifting, some of the roads are already blocked and I dare say there'll be other emergencies. They said they'd get here as fast as possible, but that could be. . .'

Beth put an arm round the older woman sympathetically. They were both shivering violently.

'Bear up, May. It may not be as bad as you think, and Jim's a tough old bird.'

'He's too old for this sort of thing,' she said roughly as she pushed open the field gate. Her eyes filled with tears. 'I'll be giving him a piece of my mind when this is all over, that's for sure.'

Beth followed blindly, the pain in her ankle almost forgotten as she pressed on. At one point she stumbled on a frozen rut. Neil's hand shot out to steady her and she couldn't help wincing as her ankle jarred.

'You shouldn't be here,' his voice rasped.

'Well, I am here, and I'm staying,' she retaliated.

He released her instantly, but not before she had seen his mouth tighten.

'He's over there.'

From a distance they could see the fallen tractor and the anxiously waiting Jason, an empty sack hugged for warmth round his shoulders.

'He's over here.'

Neil swore softly as finally they reached the man who lay pinned beneath the tractor. Throwing his bag down, he fell to his knees, breathing hard as he leaned closer to reach the man's wrist to check his pulse.

In the eerie silence May Rawlings made a small whimpering sound.

'He's still breathing.'

Beth released a sharp, pent-up breath.

'I tried to make him as comfortable as I could.' Young Jason Carter was eighteen. He looked cold and frightened—and with good reason, Beth thought as she knelt beside Neil, trying to assess the situation.

'Is there any chance of moving him?'

He shook his head, passing the back of his hand across his eyes. 'Not until we know what the full damage is. Let's get some oxygen going.'

Beth was already slipping the mask gently over the injured man's nose and mouth, warily watching the precariously angled frame of the tractor.

Neil shifted his weight until he was almost lying on

the ground. 'Blast! We could do with some extra light.'

'I've got a torch somewhere.' Reaching into her bag, Beth found a torch and directed the beam onto the injured man.

'Can you see where he's trapped?' She bent down, peering into the metal wreckage.

'No.' Neil grunted. 'Wait... Yes, it's his leg that seems to have taken most of the impact.'

Beth swallowed hard. Lowering her voice she said, 'How bad is it?'

He straightened slightly. 'It's broken and it's not a clean break. I can see the bone. There could be other crush injuries. I can't get close enough but he's lost a lot of blood. Damn this light and the cold.'

Jim Rawlings groaned.

Instinctively Beth dropped to the ground, lying flat as she stretched out a hand towards him. He was inches away, just out of reach. She shuffled her body lower, starting as Neil's hand closed, steel-like, over her arm.

'What the hell do you think you're doing?'

'I can get to him.' She dashed flakes of snow from her hair.

He lowered his voice grimly. 'You're not going in there, Beth. That tractor could shift at any minute.'

'All the more reason to reach him before it does,' she snapped. 'There's just about room for me, and we're wasting time. You said yourself that he's lost a lot of blood and he's in pain.'

Jim Rawlings cried out. She heard Neil's muttered expletive and then, before she could utter a protest, he was lying flat on the snow-covered ground, edging beneath the metal frame.

With an exclamation she fumbled for the torch, focussing it on the injured man. For the first time she could see his features clearly. At sixty years old, he was thin and wiry. His greying hair was matted with blood from a head wound, and he was clearly in deep shock. His breathing was shallow and uneven.

Above them the metal wreckage groaned and shifted slightly. She held her breath.

'Try not to move, Jim,' Neil said evenly.

'What. . .what happened?'

'You've had an accident. The tractor overturned. I'm just going to give you something for the pain.' As he spoke, surprisingly calmly, Neil held out a hand towards her, taking the syringe she had shakily prepared in readiness. He looked haggard, she thought.

The tension was getting to all of them. 'This is morphine, Jim. It should make you feel drowsy,' she heard Neil explain quietly before he edged his way further under the tractor. 'We're going to try to get you out, but first we have to find out just where you're injured so that we don't do more damage.'

Jim Rawlings moistened his lips with his tongue. 'Can't feel my leg.'

'It's broken, Jim. I'm just going to. . .' Neil eased his weight '. . .check you over so that we know where the damage is. Dr Maitland is here with me and the ambulance is on its way. With any luck, we'll have you out of here and in hospital before you know it.'

'May?' He tried to move his head and groaned.

'I'm here, Jim.' His wife knelt briefly beside him. 'I'm staying with you.' She glanced at Beth, then stood back, shaking.

'Can you tell me where it hurts, Jim?' Neil asked.

He opened his eyes and seemed to consider. 'Chest.'

'All right. Don't try to move.' He grasped the other man's free hand reassuringly. 'The injection should start working fairly quickly. Try to relax. We'll soon have you out.'

He eased herself out from beneath the wreckage and Beth held her breath as he struggled to his feet, breathing hard.

'Are you all right?'

'I'm fine. I wish I could say the same for the patient.' He frowned. 'Apart from the leg, I'd guess he has several broken ribs and there's rigidity in the upper abdomen on the left side.'

Beth drew a harsh breath. 'You think his spleen could be ruptured?'

'It's possible. I've managed to put a pressure pad on the leg wound but, otherwise, I'm reluctant to make any attempt to move him until the paramedics and the fire brigade get here.'

'How bad is it?' May Rawlings was shivering violently, as much, Beth realised, from shock as from the cold. She put an arm gently round the woman's shoulders, aware as she did so of a feeling of relief as she saw the distant flashing blue lights of the approaching ambulance.

'He's lost quite a lot of blood,' she said quietly. 'His leg is broken and so are several ribs. We're not sure if his spleen is affected.' She heard the woman's tiny gasp of terror.

'The ambulance is here, May,' Neil said gently. 'Just hold on. Jim will be in hospital in no time.'

'I'm going with him.'

'Yes, of course.'

Neil was already heading for the approaching vehicle. In the flashing blue lights his features looked haggard. Beth watched as he spoke quickly to the paramedics and the fire-service officers. Suddenly there were people everywhere, and she stood watching as Jim Rawlings was finally lifted gently and expertly on board the ambulance, his wife climbing in beside him.

Crazily, it was only then that reaction seemed to set in and she felt herself shaking uncontrollably. Suddenly she felt cold and tired and her ankle was throbbing. She straightened her back, easing the muscles, and felt Neil's arm come round her shoulders.

'Come on. I'm taking you home,' he said grimly.

'I should go to the hospital. . .' She felt the muscles in his arm tense.

'There's nothing you can do, Beth. He's in the best possible hands. The best thing you can do is to get out of those wet clothes before you get pneumonia.'

'And what about you? You look awful.' She stared up at him, anger suddenly—illogically—welling up. 'I suppose you realise you could have been killed out there?' she snapped.

'Thanks.' His mouth twisted. 'I'm big and strong.'

And wasn't that the truth? she thought, suddenly glad of his arm around her as they made their way unsteadily back to the car.

The drive to the cottage seemed to take for ever. She sat slumped in her seat, trying desperately to shut out a growing awareness of the man beside her. She found herself wondering how she would have coped if he hadn't been there. Like it or not, it seemed that Neil Quinn had become a consideration in her life, and she found the thought more than a little disconcerting.

He cut the engine and she tried to find the energy to move and get out of the car. Neil sat beside her, his eyes closed, making no attempt to do so.

'I'll make coffee,' she ventured finally. 'I think we could both use some, don't you? One way or another, it's been quite a day.'

He turned his head to look at her. 'It's getting late.'

She shivered, and instantly he was all concern. 'You're cold.'

Cold was only part of it. Her emotions seemed to be in a state of turmoil. It was probably delayed shock, she told herself. But that didn't explain her sudden reluctance to climb out of the car—to move away from the sensations his nearness aroused—and say good-night. Yes, it was definitely shock.

She swallowed hard, resting her head back against the seat. 'I hope Jim is going to be all right. He and May have worked darned hard to keep that farm going.' She turned her head to look at him. 'They had a son, Steve. Jim always had this idea that one day he'd hand everything over, lock, stock and barrel.'

Neil said quietly, without looking at her, 'That's probably how it is with most farms. They pass from generation to generation, sometimes staying in the same family for centuries.'

She stared out of the windscreen, aware of a sudden feeling of helplessness. 'Steve was killed. He'd just bought himself a new motorbike. He was crazy about them. Apparently, he collided with a lorry. That was it, all over in a few seconds.'

Neil's face was grim as he reached out for her, and a sob caught in her throat. 'Don't, Beth. Don't.'

She stared at him, swallowing hard. 'It all seems so unfair. A lifetime's work—wasted.'

'Jim Rawlings may not agree with you.'

Her chin lifted. 'And what about May? No one asked her. She lost her son. This afternoon she almost lost her husband.'

His hands closed over her arms. 'Hey, come on. You're tired. You're not thinking rationally.'

He was right—she was tired. It had been a long, fraught day and suddenly his nearness wasn't helping. What she needed more than anything right now was to be in his arms. But what would it solve? She drew herself up sharply.

Blast the man! Why had he come walking into her life, filling it with complications and making her feel vulnerable?

In desperation she tried to move away, and sensed a tightening of his muscles.

'Beth.' His voice was very soft. 'The Rawlings probably wouldn't have done anything differently, even if they'd known. Farming is their life. It's what they've been brought up to do. Jim's a strong man. He'll get over this and he'll carry on. We have to do the same. We're doctors—we can't tell people how to live their lives.'

He moved to kiss her very gently, his lips brushing against hers, yet it was enough to make her feel as if her body was on fire.

She found herself gazing in rapt fascination as his face loomed closer, bringing with it the utterly sensuous mouth. Involuntarily she closed her eyes, then her head went back as she let herself be swept along on a confusing tide of emotions.

Desire flared out of control. She moaned softly and her hands reached up, drawing him closer. She moved restlessly, searching for some kind of fulfilment that seemed only just out of reach.

'I want you, Beth,' he rasped, breathing against the soft fullness of her mouth as his hands caressed the curve of her breast.

She gasped at the shaft of exquisite pleasure his touch sent coursing through her, bringing with it a sudden and completely new kind of awareness.

With an overwhelming sense of shock, she realised that she was within a hair's breadth of falling in love with this man. It would take very little to make it happen

if she was prepared to let it. But what then? She had
been down this particular road before. Could she bear
to go through it all again?

Her breath caught in her throat. She had promised
herself, after James's betrayal, that she would never
let herself feel like this again—never allow herself to
become vulnerable. But, then, a tiny inner voice rose
to taunt her, she had never felt like this with James.

For a second shock left her swaying, then she was
struggling to break free. Everything was happening too
fast. 'I. . . It's getting late,' she said breathlessly.

She heard his sharp intake of breath. 'Beth, what is
it? What's wrong?'

She tried to turn away but, frustratingly, his grip
merely tightened. He looked at her, his dark gaze
narrowing. 'You must know I'd never hurt you.'

She drew a ragged breath. 'It's all happening too
fast. I'm confused. I can't. . .I'm not sure I can go
through this again.'

Suddenly one hand was beneath her chin, forcing her
to look at him. 'There was someone?'

'I thought so,' she said steadily. 'His name
was James.'

A brief hardness flared in his eyes. 'Can you talk
about it?'

'There isn't much to tell.' She swallowed hard. 'We
weren't even officially engaged. Maybe I expected too
much, or misread the signs.'

'Somehow I doubt that.'

She looked away. 'I was a medical student. James
had qualified a couple of years ahead of me.' Suddenly
she found herself talking quite calmly. 'We seemed to
have a lot in common—the same interests, the same
circle of friends.'

A spasm flickered across Neil's face. 'What went wrong?' he asked quietly.

She shifted restlessly as his persistent probing began to stir memories she had imagined were safely buried. 'I'm still not sure. Maybe we just grew up and grew apart. As I said, we weren't even officially engaged. It was just that everyone assumed. . .' She paused momentarily as words failed her.

'I suppose I was spending a lot of time studying. Too much maybe, but it meant a lot to me to qualify. James. . .' She tucked a strand of hair behind her ear. 'He needed to be at the centre of things. That's not his fault—it's the way he was.'

She bit at her lower lip. 'Maybe I just didn't see what was happening. He began to. . .resent the fact that I couldn't always be there. Eventually, one day he told me he'd met someone else. It was as simple as that.' Except that the someone else had been her best friend. She looked at Neil, sensing his anger as he muttered something beneath his breath. Her fingers clenched.

'Did you love him?' he asked.

'I thought so at the time. Obviously I was mistaken.'

His thumb gently traced the outline of her mouth. 'These things happen. It wasn't your fault, Beth. Sometimes we just have to learn to let go.'

But was that what he had done? Wasn't he still holding onto the memory of his wife?

'You make it sound so easy.'

'No,' he said, frowning. 'It's never that.'

She was beginning to lose control beneath the feather-light touch of his fingers against her cheek and eyes. She stood very still, her eyes closed, afraid he might see what was happening to her. She had imagined she loved James. She knew now that she had been fooling herself. Her feelings for James bore no relation to what she was experiencing now with this man.

She tensed with the need to resist the powerful feelings he was evoking. There was no future in it. It was all so unfair.

In desperation she drew away. 'I. . .I'm really very tired. We both need some sleep.'

He looked at her, his gaze narrowed. 'Maybe you're right. It's time I left.' His voice was rough-edged as he draped her coat round her shoulders, the pressure of his hands lingering just a shade too long for her peace of mind.

Safely inside the cottage, she closed the door firmly behind her and stood with her head resting against it, hearing him drive away.

She sighed heavily as she straightened up, vaguely aware of Henry coming to greet her. He followed her, tail swishing and rubbing himself against her legs, as she moved into the kitchen and opened the fridge door to gaze at the contents.

'Yes, I'm pleased to see you, too,' she murmured, stroking his fur in a motion that at any other time would have had a soothing effect. But right now life suddenly seemed to be full of complications.

'You're tired,' she told herself aloud. So what was new? She'd been tired before. Neil Quinn was what was new.

CHAPTER FIVE

DRIVING to the surgery next morning, Beth found herself dreading the inevitable meeting with Neil. She felt tired and looked it, and a cup of strong black coffee and a couple of aspirins at breakfast hadn't helped.

She had woken feeling exhausted and hollow-eyed and, as a result of her tossing and turning, there were shadows beneath her eyes. Her face, when she'd looked in the mirror, had been so pale that she had resorted to a hint of blusher on her cheeks, before making her way, with uncharacteristic reluctance, to the surgery.

She pulled into the car park just as Neil was getting out of his own car. She sat and purposely foraged in her bag, hoping he would go in ahead of her. But he was holding the front door open when she finally got out of her car and ran lightly up the steps. She was surprised to see that he had Jamie with him.

'Hello, there.' She smiled down at him. 'How are you today?'

Pink-cheeked, Jamie eagerly tucked one small hand into her own, walking with her as Neil held the swing doors open. 'I'm going to school. I've got my lunch box.'

'So I see.' She glanced at Neil. 'Running a little late this morning, are we?'

'You could say,' he growled. 'Actually, Sally usually does the school run, but she has a dental appointment so I thought I'd pop in to see if there are any urgent messages before I drop Jamie off.' He paused to steer his son in the direction of Reception. 'I should be back

90

in plenty of time for surgery. By the way, how's the ankle?'

'Fine, thanks.' It was true. Apart from a slight ache, it was almost back to normal.

His blue eyes glinted. 'Perhaps I should check it over for you. Just to be on safe side.'

'Don't push your luck,' she retorted.

'Coward!' he murmured derisively.

He may be right at that, she thought crossly. It was difficult enough, struggling to come to terms with her physical response to him and the memories it brought. The last thing she needed right now was a reminder of her own weakness where he was concerned.

Colour darkened her cheeks as she ducked under his arm and marched briskly ahead of him. A funny sound, which might have been a cough—or could have been a chuckle—came from him. She didn't stop to find out which as she headed in the direction of the office.

'It looks as if the snow's starting to clear at last.' Ruth looked up, smiling, as she sorted through the morning mail. 'These are for you. More of the usual, from the look of it.'

'Thanks.' Beth accepted the pile of letters and grimaced wryly at the list of patients and visits. 'Looks as if it's going to be a busy one. Any sign of Alex yet?'

'In his room.'

There was a slight edge to the older woman's voice as she said it, and Beth glanced up from sifting through the bundle of cards.

'Is something wrong?'

'Well, personally, I think he'd be better off at home in bed. Preferably taking the advice he'd give to any patient who has a heavy cold. But, then, I'm only the practice manager. What would I know?' Ruth sniffed

disdainfully so that Beth had to struggle hard to keep
a straight face.

'Oh, dear, as bad as that? Perhaps I'd better pop in
and see him before I make a start.'

'I wish you luck. I think you're going to need it.
They say doctors always make the worst patients.'

'Yes, well,' Beth smiled wryly. 'I'll see if I can
talk some sense into him. Thanks, Ruth. Give me five
minutes and I'll make a start.'

'Oh, by the way, you haven't forgotten the party,
have you? I spoke to John. He's on the committee
so he has to arrive early, but I'll pick you up about
seven-thirty, if that's all right.'

Beth turned to look at her with a sinking feeling.
'Party?'

'Yes. You know, to launch the new hospital radio
service.' Ruth beamed.' Neil's going, aren't you?'

'I certainly am. Wouldn't miss it for anything.'

Beth experienced a sense of shock as she realised
that her early warning system—that tiny nervous tin-
gling that ran down her spine—had let her down as
she glanced over her shoulder to see him standing there
with Jamie at his side.

His gaze slanted over her, the blue eyes glimmering
in a way that was thoroughly disconcerting. 'You *are*
going?' he murmured with wry amusement. 'I do feel
it's important to support these things.'

Her chin rose. 'Yes, of course. I think the hospital
radio service is a wonderful idea—'

'Good. In that case, I'll see you later.'

Jamie tugged at his father's sleeve. 'Daddy, why
can't Beff come for a ride with us? I *want* her to come.'

There was a rare note of petulance in the child's
voice, and she felt the warm colour invade her cheeks
as Neil's frowning gaze seemed to linger momentarily

on her. She preferred not to guess what he must be thinking.

Swallowing hard, she bent to ruffle Jamie's hair. 'I don't think that's a good idea right now, sweetheart. I have to do some work. Another time, maybe.' Straightening, she moistened her dry lips with her tongue. 'Yes, well, I think I'd better get on.'

Neil's gaze narrowed briefly before he glanced at his watch and said, 'So, I'll see you later, then?' Without waiting for a reply, he walked away.

So much for the early night she had been promising herself, she thought as, sighing, she glanced at her own watch and gave a tiny yelp of dismay. 'Oh, Lord,' She turned to Ruth. 'I'll just see Alex first, then I'll get started.'

She sped along the corridor to tap at his door. 'Hi,' She popped her head round, just in time to see him sneeze into a large handkerchief. 'I was going to ask how you are, but I'll save myself the trouble. Alex, you look awful. What are you doing here?'

'Lot of paperwork to catch up on,' he croaked hoarsely. 'Damn stuff's never-ending.'

'Well, for heaven's sake, take it home with you, if you feel you must. Take a couple of days off. Go to bed.'

He waited for a spasm of coughing to pass. 'Nice thought, but we're up to our eyes—'

'Alex, I hate to tell you this but you're not entirely indispensable. We'll cope.' She looked at him and felt a pang of real concern. 'Have you taken your temperature?'

'Don't need to. It's up.'

'How's the throat?'

He groaned. 'Don't ask.'

'And the chest?' He didn't bother to answer. She

shook her head. 'Honestly, Alex, you look like death warmed up. Not exactly a good advert, are you? I mean it—go home. Take some aspirin and don't come back until you feel better. Neil and I can cope. It was, after all, one of the reasons why we took on a new partner.'

He rose unsteadily to his feet, reaching for his jacket. 'Well, if you're sure.'

'Absolutely, and I'll take these.' She relieved him of a pile of letters. 'Anything I can't cope with I'm sure Ruth will.'

'If there's anything really urgent—'

'We'll be sure to call, but I doubt if there's anything that can't wait a couple of days or so.' She ushered him gently towards the door. 'Don't worry, and try to *relax*. Watch television. Get plenty of rest.'

Now, there's a nice idea, she thought as minutes later she sped into her consulting room, hung up her coat and jammed her hand down hard on the bell to summon her first patient.

The door opened. 'Ah, Mr Duncan. How's that elbow of yours? Did the steroid injection work?'

The rest of the morning passed routinely with the usual batch of verrucas, sore throats and backaches. Beth looked up, smiling, as the last of her patients came hesitantly into the room.

'Hello, Mr Sampson. How are you today?'

'Not so well, Doctor.' Sixty-four-year-old Ian Sampson smiled wanly as he eased himself breathlessly into the chair. He pressed a hand to his chest. 'Can't seem to get my breath this past couple of days.'

Quickly glancing at the notes on her screen, Beth was already on her feet and reaching for her stethoscope. Even from where she stood she could hear the deep, wheezing sounds of someone with a history of

COADs—chronic obstruction of the airways disease. 'Let's have a listen to your chest and see if we can find out what's going on. You are taking your regular medicine?'

He nodded.

'Any chest pain?' she queried, as she made her examination.

He shook his head. 'Just a bit of a cough, that's all.'

'Why didn't you call me? You know I'd come out to see you any time.'

'I don't like to be any bother.'

Listening to the bubbling, chesty sounds, Beth felt her spirits drop. Thoroughly, but as quickly as possible, she made her examination. Having checked his blood pressure and heart rhythm, she straightened and smiled reassuringly.

'I don't think it's anything too serious. You've certainly got a bit of an infection, but I'll give you a course of antibiotics and hopefully it should clear up fairly quickly.'

She printed out the prescription and signed it. 'There we are. In the meantime, carry on with your usual medication and we'll see if we can ease the breathing for you. With luck, you should be feeling much better in a couple of days.'

Ian Sampson's eyes brightened visibly. 'I'm grateful, Doctor, and I know the wife will be pleased, too. She gets herself into a bit of a state when I'm not feeling too well.'

She smiled. 'I suppose that's understandable. How is Emily?'

'Not so bad. Those pills you gave her seem to be doing the trick for her arthritis. She missed being able to potter in the garden.'

'That's what we're here for. Oh, and come back to

see me if you're not feeling better after a couple of days on those tablets.'

She saw him out, before returning to tidy her desk. It was already late morning and she had several visits to make. Lunch would have to be a quick cup of coffee and a biscuit, she thought resignedly. If she was lucky.

She did a hasty recount of her patients' cards as a tap came at the door. Frowning, she glanced at her watch.

'Can you spare a minute?' Neil spoke from the open doorway. He was carrying his jacket slung over one shoulder and, now that she looked at him more closely, she realised that his casually styled black hair looked as if it had been recently trimmed.

She had to resist an almost compulsive yet totally illogical desire to run her fingers through the shorter locks to ruffle its neatness.

She scooped up a pile of magazines. 'Actually, I'm running a bit late. I've a few calls to make. . .'

'I just thought you'd like to know that Jim Rawlings is more comfortable this morning. I rang the hospital and they reckon he's going to be OK.'

'Oh, that's wonderful news.'

'It's going to take time, and a lot of hard work on his part, but it could have been a lot worse.'

'I'm so glad.' She dropped her stethoscope and diary into her briefcase. 'I've been worrying about May.'

'I had an idea you might be.' Neil raised an amused eyebrow. 'That's why I checked up. At least now you can stop worrying.'

If only all her problems were so easily solved. She stifled a sigh and felt a small pulse hammer in her throat as Neil's gaze swept over her, taking in the classic lines of her straight, knee-length skirt and the soft, cream-coloured silk shirt beneath her jacket.

He was doing it again, she thought, wandering into

her mind like an uninvited guest. Neil Quinn was definitely a distracting influence.

She slammed her briefcase closed decisively. 'Oh, by the way, I persuaded Alex to go home. He won't admit to it, but he's got a chest infection. I told him to stay away until he's feeling better.' She glanced up at him, frowning. 'I hope that's all right. I should have checked with you first. . .'

'You did what you thought best,' he said easily. 'As a matter of fact, I spoke to him about it yesterday. I tried to talk him out of coming in. Obviously you speak with the voice of authority.'

'I doubt it.' She gave a slight laugh. 'I think he was just feeling like death and decided to give in gracefully.' She hauled her briefcase more firmly into her grasp.

Neil reached the door ahead of her and held it open, but made no attempt to let her pass. 'I didn't ask if you're all right. I've been meaning to. . .'

'Me?' She frowned.

'I just wondered,' he said evenly. 'After what happened yesterday.'

Was he being funny? She stared intently at the attractive planes of his face, looking for some signs of amusement at her expense. His mouth was nerve-shatteringly sensual.

She drew herself up sharply. 'Yes, of course I am,' she said edgily. 'Why wouldn't I be?'

His dark eyebrows rose quizzically. 'It was a nasty accident. Probably made worse by the fact that you knew the person involved. I thought you might be suffering some sort of delayed shock.'

She drew a deep breath. The only kind of shock she was suffering was from the effect his nearness always seemed to have on her nervous system. 'I'm fine. Look, I really do have to get on. . .'

Moments later she was on her way out through the now almost empty waiting room when Ruth called her back.

'Beth, we've just had a late call. I thought you might want to take it. It was Mrs Dawson.'

'Becky?' She came to a halt, frowning. 'Did she say what the problem is?'

'Only that she's a bit worried about the baby.' Ruth handed her a slip of paper. 'I gather she's still snuffly and running a bit of a temperature. I said you'd fit the call in this afternoon, if that's all right.'

'Yes, I'll pop over there as soon as I can. See you later.'

It was raining outside as Beth finally set off to make her calls. Consulting her list, she headed away from the coast and travelled inland to one of the new housing estates which had begun to spring up over the past couple of years.

The patient turned out to be a fractious five-year-old with a runny nose and spots.

'I'm sorry to call you out, Doctor,' the anxious, heavily pregnant mother said as she ushered Beth into the sitting room where a young boy lay huddled in a chair. She eased her back. 'I just didn't think I could make it all the way to the surgery, especially as Robert's being so uncooperative. It's a struggle at the best of times.'

'Don't worry about it.' Beth smiled. 'When's the baby due?'

'A week ago.' Jenny Lucas smiled wryly. 'As far as I'm concerned, the sooner it puts in an appearance the better.' She paused at the door. 'It's not like Robert to be so quiet and miserable. He's usually such a happy little chap.'

'In my experience, when a normally lively child is

quiet it's usually a sure sign that something is wrong. It's the noisy ones we don't worry too much about. So—hello, young man.' She put her briefcase down and sat on the edge of the chair, already making a swift, professional assessment of the flushed and restless child. 'Mummy says you're not feeling too well.'

Taking a spatula from her briefcase, she took one small hand in her own. 'Can I take a look at your throat to see if there are any nasty germs?'

In fact, it scarcely needed an examination to confirm an advanced case of tonsillitis, but she made the usual investigations, before straightening up. 'The poor little chap has got tonsillitis and a slight ear infection, too.'

'Oh, no. Poor Rob. But what about the rash? I was half-afraid it might be measles.'

'No, it definitely isn't measles.' Beth smiled reassuringly as she wrote out a prescription. 'With any kind of infection, the temperature is usually raised. Some children seem to react by coming out in a kind of heat rash. It doesn't usually cause any problems, but if he feels a bit itchy you could dab a spot of cooling lotion on it.

'I'm going to give you an antibiotic. It has quite a pleasant flavour so you shouldn't have too much trouble getting him to take it. But do finish the whole course. Give him plenty of fluids, and don't worry too much if he doesn't feeling like eating for a couple of days.' She smiled.

'They usually make up for it later. So, young man. . .' she ruffled the sleepy child's hair '. . .I hope you'll soon be feeling better.'

Getting to her feet, she followed Jenny Lucas to the door. 'If you're at all worried or if he doesn't seem to be feeling better in a few days either give me a call or bring him to the surgery. Oh, and good luck with the baby, by the way.'

It was mid-afternoon and the light was already beginning to fade by the time Beth had finished her calls and finally headed towards the Dawsons' cottage.

Knocking at the door, she chafed her hands and shivered as the afternoon temperature began to drop— heralding another frost.

Becky answered within seconds, holding the crying baby—wrapped in a shawl—in her arms. She greeted Beth's arrival with a sigh of relief. 'Oh, thank heavens. Come in. Do you fancy a coffee? I could do with one. I'm at my wit's end. Hannah's been crying almost non-stop for the past two hours.'

Beth followed her friend into the kitchen. 'Here, let me take the baby for a few minutes,' she volunteered, shedding her coat. 'Why don't you switch the kettle on and tell me what's wrong?'

Becky flipped the switch on the kettle, spooned coffee into mugs and sank into a chair to rest her head in her hands. 'I hardly got any sleep last night. I'm *exhausted*. She just keeps crying, Beth, and I don't know what to do. I've tried everything.'

'Look, sit and drink your coffee while I take a look at her. Has she been taking her feeds?'

'No, not really.'

'Hmm. She does still sound a bit snuffly.' Beth gently took off the baby's matinée coat before reaching into her briefcase for her stethoscope.

'Yes, she is.' Becky watched anxiously, her hands wrapped round the mug of coffee, as Beth listened to the baby's chest.

'How old is she now? Nearly two weeks?'

Becky nodded.

'And how about her weight? Is she still gaining?'

'She was doing fine. But I'm worried that she hasn't been taking her feeds properly this past couple of days. She seems hungry but then she pulls away and gets grizzly. Or she just seems to want to sleep. I mean, I know babies do, but. . .'

Beth coiled her stethoscope, dropping it back into her case before lying the baby across her knees. Carefully she examined the tiny throat for enlarged glands and then, with her auroscope, checked the baby's ears.

'What is it?' Becky pushed her coffee-mug away. 'What's wrong with her, Beth? It's not serious, is it?'

Gently Beth refastened the matinée coat, before lifting the baby against her shoulder. She brushed her fingers through the soft, downy hair.

'No, I don't think it's anything serious.' She smiled reassuringly. 'She *is* a little bit chesty, and she does have a slight temperature. You might find that tepid sponging will help bring it down or, if that doesn't work, you can give her a small dose of Calpol.'

'But why is she so grizzly?'

'Well, she's obviously a bit poorly and she's probably hungry but because her nose is blocked she isn't able to feed properly. Can you get her to take some boiled water?'

'I can try. She isn't very keen.'

Beth smiled. 'Even a few drops at a time will help. It's important to keep up her fluid intake.'

'I feel so guilty, calling you out.'

'There's no need. You did absolutely the right thing.' She moved the baby to her other shoulder, smelling the sweet, baby smell of her and feeling the velvety softness of the small cheek against her own.

'Makes you feel broody, doesn't it?' Becky gave a

tired grin. 'Dangerous things, babies. I've heard they're catching.'

'That's a new one on me.' Beth smiled. All the same, she felt her heart give a jolt as she craned her neck to gaze at the tiny scrap, nuzzling at her face, and felt her throat tighten spasmodically at the sudden realisation that she *wanted* a child of her own—to feel it growing inside her.

She tried to imagine it, laughing and dark-haired.

Her eyes widened in shock. Now, why on earth should she think that? She closed her eyes briefly on a tantalising image of Neil Quinn and felt suddenly, ridiculously, vulnerable as she clutched the baby to her.

Taking a deep breath, she handed the baby briskly back to her friend. 'Don't ever take risks with a baby. Far better safe than sorry. Look, I'm going to give you a prescription for some antibiotics. I think she has a slight chest infection and we don't want it to get any worse.'

She wrote out a prescription, leaving it on the kitchen table. 'In the meantime, keep trying to get some fluids into her and bring her to see me at the surgery in a few days' time just so that I can check her over again.' She grinned. 'Apart from anything else, it will give me a good excuse to have another cuddle. If you're worried about her before then give me a call straight away.'

'I can't tell you how grateful I am.' Becky gave a slight smile. 'I've been so worried—a regular doting mother. You must see it all the time.'

'It's the most natural thing in the world to feel concerned.' Beth snapped the locks on her briefcase. 'How's George?'

'Tired, but bearing up. Look, we never seem to get the time for a chat these days.'

Beth looked ruefully at her watch and sighed. 'Oh,

Becky, I'd love to stay but I'd better get back. I've still got some paperwork to do.' And she still hadn't even given a thought to what she was going to wear tonight.

She made her way to the door. 'We'll have to get together properly soon and have a real gossip. You're right, it's been ages. Don't forget to pop into the surgery in a few days.'

It was late afternoon and freezing again by the time she had completed the paperwork, made several telephone calls and written a letter of referral to a consultant. It wasn't until she was driving back along the coast road that she realised she was actually tired, and a niggling tension headache was beginning to make its presence felt.

The last thing she needed was to be going out again, having to make polite conversation, when all she really wanted was a shower, some food and an early night.

She fed Henry, made herself a cup of strong, black coffee, nibbled at a biscuit and took herself to the bathroom to indulge in a soak in her favourite foaming bath oil.

An hour later her hair was freshly shampooed and needed nothing more than blow-drying. Deliberating in front of the mirror over whether to put it up or leave it loose, she decided on the latter, and brushed it until the chestnut waves shone.

Her make-up she applied slightly more heavily than she would have worn during the day, with silver-grey shadow adding emphasis to her eyes, a touch of blusher for her cheeks and lipstick.

Clad in fresh satin undies, she was fastening a delicate gold chain around her neck when she heard the arrival of a car and seconds later a ring at the doorbell.

'Let yourself in, Ruth,' she called out. 'I'll be with

you in a minute. Help yourself to coffee or a fruit juice.'

She heard the door open and close again. Small, gold hoop earrings caught the light as she turned her head and stepped into the knee-length black dress she had finally decided to wear.

For a second doubts came rushing in. Was it a little too startling? Too short, maybe? As she moved the fabric clung to her hips, emphasising her dark-stockinged legs.

As she eased herself carefully into the bodice it clung to her breasts as if it had been moulded to her, a thin, diamanté halter giving an illusion of safety—except that the illusion was too swiftly shattered. The zip had somehow stuck.

Craning her neck to look in the mirror, she gave a sigh of annoyance as she saw that it had somehow managed to tangle with the fabric. Damn! Well, there was only one thing for it.

She eased it down again, slipped her feet into high-heeled sandals, sprayed a delicate mist of her favourite perfume behind her ears and, clutching the unfastened bodice to her, hurried downstairs.

'Ruth, I'm so sorry to have kept you waiting. I've had a minor disaster. I wonder if you'd mind zipping—'

She broke off, feeling a rush of heat and cold all at the same time as Neil studied her with penetrating intensity. She felt the glittering sweep of his blue eyes flame over the creamy translucence of her bare shoulders and the curve of her breasts.

'You!' She swallowed convulsively on the sudden tightness in her throat. 'But I. . .I was expecting Ruth.'

'Sorry to disappoint you,' he said evenly. 'Something came up. A minor panic, something to do with the refreshments. Ruth felt she should be there so I offered to pick you up instead.' Beth wondered if she had imagined the note of satisfaction in his voice. 'It looks as if I arrived at just the right moment. Can I help?'

CHAPTER SIX

BETH passed her tongue over her dry lips, intensely aware of Neil and the musky tang of his aftershave. 'I see. Well, in that case. . .'

Heat flooded through her body as he slowly drew up the zip on her dress, his fingers brushing against her skin in the process. If she had thought him attractive before, he was devastatingly so now in the more formal dark suit.

'There you go. All safe and sound.'

She moved away, feeling oddly breathless and glad to put some distance between them. She stood, frowning, in the open doorway. 'Can I offer you a drink before we go? There's some sherry—' She broke off, something in the glittering gaze that raked her slowly from head to toe making her hesitate.

Panic hit her. She stared down at her dress, blushing as she remembered how little she was wearing beneath it. 'Is something wrong? With. . .with the dress, I mean? You don't think it's too short?' She licked her lips again. 'I could go and change. It won't take a minute. . .'

'You look beautiful,' he said huskily. 'I think we'll forget the drink.' He draped the small, matching jacket round her shoulders, his hands briefly making contact with her flesh.

She glanced anxiously at her watch. 'I'm sorry. I should have been ready. I didn't realise we were late.'

His gaze narrowed as he held the door open. 'We're not—yet,' he said tautly.

106

Beth swallowed hard, her breathing uneven as he ushered her towards the car. He opened the passenger door and helped her in, before going round to the driver's seat. It wasn't a small car, but he was still far too close and still the most sexually exciting man she had ever met.

An involuntary shiver ran through her and, as if instantly aware of it, he took his eyes from the road to glance at her.

'Nervous?'

She *was*, but not for the reason he was thinking! 'Not really.' She avoided his gaze, glad that he had mistaken the real reason behind that shiver. His nearness was affecting her in a way she hadn't dreamed possible.

She gave a slight smile. 'I'm still not quite sure how I managed to get roped into this. Ruth and her husband have been involved for a year or so with the hospital broadcasting service, but. . .'

'Other people's causes have a way of taking over?' Neil turned to look at her, grinning. 'I know what you mean.'

She looked at him. 'I would have thought you had the perfect excuse. I mean, you've scarcely been here long enough to become involved. What have you done with Jamie, by the way?'

'One of Sally's nieces offered to babysit. Actually, I do know a bit about the hospital radio service. I did an occasional stint at the hospital.'

She turned her head to look at him. 'What? As a DJ? You?'

He grinned. 'Oh, nothing too heavy. A light musical programme, that sort of thing. Even got to interview the odd local personality. And I use the word *odd* advisedly.' He laughed, then sobered. 'Seriously, I know how much patients, particularly long-stay ones, appreciate the hospital radio—anything that relieves the monotony, especially for those who might be bed-bound and don't find it easy to read.'

She was touched by the genuine note of enthusiasm in his voice. 'I had no idea.'

He took his eyes briefly from the road to look at her. 'There's quite a lot you don't know about me, Beth.' His mouth quirked. 'But I'm working on it,' he added softly, so softly that she wasn't even sure if he had actually said it or if she had imagined it.

The hospital lounge was already crowded by the time they arrived. Neil disappeared to hang up her jacket and she hovered uncertainly in the doorway, suddenly reluctant to become part of what seemed to have turned into a large, noisy party rather than the small social affair she had expected.

She scanned the room. Some of the faces she recognised, others she didn't. In fact, she was just beginning to wonder whether she could make a reasonably discreet withdrawal when John Baxter came up to her, brandishing a tray of glasses.

'Glad you could make it.' Tall and solidly built, in his late fifties, he raised his voice to make himself heard above the music. 'How about a glass of wine? Red or white?'

'White, please, John.' Beth accepted it gratefully, glad of something to keep her hands occupied. Neil appeared suddenly beside her, helped himself to a glass of orange juice and was instantly waylaid by a flushed, bright-eyed member of the hospital's social committee.

She sipped at her drink and looked round the room. 'Quite a turnout, isn't it? You must be pleased.'

'Great, isn't it? We didn't expect so many but it's good to see just how much support there is.' John was clearly happy. 'Have you seen Ruth?'

'No, not yet.'

'She's around somewhere—supervising food, I think she said. Or possibly the raffle. We've managed to get some important people here tonight.' He looked round the room. 'See that chap over there?' He indicated a group, huddled in a corner. 'Presenter from the local television company.'

'Really?' Beth's eyes widened in genuine surprise. 'Oh, yes, you're right. I recognise him now.'

'And the one next to him, the tall one. Local radio. He's brought several of his cronies along, too. The girl with red hair—she does an afternoon spot. You may have heard of it. *Teabreak*, they call it. News, music, a bit of a chat—that sort of thing.' He grinned. 'We recorded my bit earlier. It goes out tomorrow.'

'I'm sure it will be great. I shall listen out for it.'

'Well, I figure the more interest we can raise in hospital radio the better.'

Beth glanced around her and smiled. 'You certainly seem to have done the trick. And here was I, expecting about a dozen members of the hospital board to turn up.'

He grinned. 'Probably fancy their chances of getting their photos taken. The local press is here in force, too. See what I mean? Ah, I've just spotted Ruth. She's looking a bit harassed. Better go and rescue her.'

John sidestepped Beth just as a photographer aimed his camera in her direction and a tall figure bumped into her, almost spilling her wine.

A flash bulb went off as she stepped back, a hand shielding her eyes, and a familiar voice murmured softly, 'Careful, there. Those things are a damned nuisance. Here, better let me take that before you have an accident.'

A hand removed her glass as she mopped at the few spots that had fallen onto her dress. A dancing couple jostled for space and she was suddenly aware of Neil's body pressed against hers. She felt the tautness of his body and turned her flustered gaze up to meet his—just as the flash bulb exploded again and Neil's hand took a firm grip of her arm.

'I think perhaps we should circulate, don't you?'

He wasn't giving her any choice. Her breathing was constricted as he drew her away through the increasingly noisy press of bodies.

'Have you eaten yet?'

She shook her head. Earlier she had felt ravenously hungry, but somehow her appetite had vanished.

'You should have something. That wine can seem pretty innocuous but I wouldn't recommend it on an empty stomach.'

Beth found herself being guided expertly towards a buffet table which was laden with what seemed to be an extravagant amount of food.

'Here, have a plate.'

She toyed with flakes of pastry. He was right about the wine. It had hit her empty stomach in a rush and she was feeling distinctly light-headed. She winced as the young DJ got into his stride, turning up the volume so that the bass seemed to match the throbbing in her head.

'It's going very well, isn't it?'

'It's a good cause. One that doesn't generally seem to rate a great deal of publicity.' Neil's mouth curved. 'I suppose hospital radio isn't something you think about unless you happen to be on the receiving end.'

She looked at him slightly unsteadily. 'I still can't imagine you as a disc jockey.'

'Ah. One of my many hidden talents.' His mouth twisted in gentle mockery. 'Didn't they teach you in medical school that even doctors are allowed to be human?'

All too human, she thought as she closed her eyes, feeling the noise and heat closing in around her.

'Hey, Doc!'

Beth opened her eyes quickly as the voice intruded. One of the local reporters stood in front of them, brandishing a notebook and pencil.

'Thought I'd get a few comments from the people involved. A little local colour, so to speak.' He glanced around him. 'Must be a lot going on behind the scenes in a place like this—know what I mean? A few stories?' He grinned, and beside her Beth felt Neil stiffen.

'We'd like to help,' she said quickly, 'but I'm afraid you'd be very disappointed. There's nothing very exciting about the medical profession.'

Daniel Lacey's speculative glance moved slowly from her flushed face to that of the man beside her. 'Go on. All these good-looking doctors! I wouldn't mind betting my pension there's the odd little. . .' he made a rocking motion with his hand '. . .romance cooking behind the scenes. I've watched all the soaps on telly.' He scribbled in his notepad. 'How about you, Doc?'

Beth wasn't sure whether the odd muffled sound in Neil's throat was anger or laughter, but she was suddenly very conscious of his arm, coming to drape itself loosely round her waist.

'I never watch soap operas,' he said softly. 'I hate to be a spoilsport, but I believe the customary response in answer to personal questions is "no comment". Suddenly his grip tightened and he was smiling down at her. "Isn't that right, darling? We have no statement to make yet.'

Beth's shocked gaze flew up to meet his and she saw

teasing laughter in his eyes. She thought about breaking away from his grasp, only to feel herself drawn closer still and—even as her lips parted in protest—his mouth came down over hers in a kiss that held her rooted to the spot.

She knew precisely what he was doing and it was working, she could see as she forced her eyes open and saw the gleam of triumph in the eyes of the watching reporter. She had no idea how long the kiss lasted. It was probably only seconds before she managed to break away, but it left her feeling as if she had been hit by a tidal wave.

Daniel Lacey closed his notebook with a satisfied flourish. 'Well, I'll take it I can quote that relations are definitely friendly. Thanks for your co-operation, folks. I'll see you around.' He ambled away, in search of another victim, no doubt, she thought as she glared furiously at Neil.

'How *could* you?' She reached for her glass and drank her wine far too quickly. She choked furiously and he patted her back. 'Don't do that.' She pulled away. 'I'm very angry and, besides, I think you've played to the cameras and press sufficiently already, don't you?'

'I couldn't resist it.' He smiled.

'Obviously not.' She felt like crying with humiliation and a whole lot of other emotions she didn't even want to define. 'I'm only surprised you didn't offer to let him take pictures.'

'It didn't occur to me,' he said quietly. 'In any case, that wasn't what I meant.' He handed her his handkerchief and she mopped at a spot of wine on her dress, catching a faint whiff of his aftershave as she did so.

'You enjoyed every minute of it.' She glared as she thrust the handkerchief back at him.

'Well, I can't deny that,' he said softly, and she knew that if she didn't move she would end up in his arms again. 'I really think we should dance, don't you?'

'Dance?'

'I get the feeling it might be expected.' He stared down at her and her pulse rate accelerated dangerously as he took her in his arms, moving slowly rather than attempting to dance apart. 'Don't be cross,' he murmured softly, his lips brushing against her hair.

'I'm only surprised you didn't make some personal statement which he could have quoted in his miserable excuse for a newspaper.'

'You're taking it too much to heart,' he said soberly. "I've had some experience of dealing with the press. Most are thoroughly honest and genuine. Some—a few—make their own rules. The more you try to avoid them, refuse to answer their questions, the more tenacious they become. Anyway. . .' he grinned, 'imagine how annoyed he's going to be when he realises we don't even work at the hospital.'

Her chin rose. 'I thought I was handling things quite well. Politely but firmly. . .'

'Believe me,' he drawled softly, 'you would have been way out of your depth.'

But, then, wasn't she already? The pressure of Neil's hand on her back moulded her body to his, and a tiny tremor ran through her.

He glanced at his watch. 'We've put in an appearance. I think we could safely bow out now, don't you?'

'Oh, I thought it was still early.' Perversely she felt disappointed.

He grimaced ruefully. 'It's after ten-thirty. Alex is holding the fort. I wasn't expecting any emergencies, but I said I'd take over again at midnight.'

He had somehow deftly managed to manoeuvre her

to where Ruth and John were standing with a group of hospital dignitaries.

'I'm afraid we have to love and leave you.' Neil leaned forward to kiss Ruth who laughed coyly, her face flushed with pleasure. 'It's been a great evening, but I promised Alex I'd take over from him. We'll collect our coats on the way out.' He shook hands with John. 'Congratulations on the launch. I know the service will be much appreciated.'

Before she knew it Beth found herself in the car, and Neil was climbing in beside her. He made a few perfunctory remarks, but apart from that drove in silence. It was a relief. It gave her a chance to stare out of the window and try to put her thoughts in order. Except that it didn't seem to work.

She wasn't aware she had sighed until his gaze drifted briefly in the semi-darkness from the road to her face.

'Tired?'

'Mmm.' She smiled ruefully. 'It was a good evening. I'm glad for John's sake that so many people turned up. Everyone seemed to have a good time. I think I've just forgotten how to be a social animal, that's all.'

'It's easy to fall out of the habit,' he said quietly.

She turned to look at him and almost wished she hadn't as his hand brushed against her arm, sending a range of ill-timed signals firing through her. 'You seem to manage.'

'Certain obligations go with the job,' he said. 'No one said we have to enjoy it.'

She darted a glance at his profile. Even in the darkness she could see the tension in his features. She swallowed hard. 'I'm sorry, I didn't mean to. . .'

'Beth, it's all right. I can think of Louise—mention

her name. Just because someone has gone doesn't mean you forget.'

The car came to a halt and he switched off the engine. It wasn't until she gazed out of the window that she even realised she was home.

'It can't have been easy,' she said uncertainly. 'Moving away from everything you've been used to. You must miss her.'

He stared ahead through the windscreen, making no attempt to move. 'What I miss is knowing that when I walk through the door someone will be there. But most of all I know that Jamie is the one who's missed out. Kids should have mothers.' He turned to look at her, his voice taut. 'There are days when I can't even remember what she looked like. Does that sound awful?'

Unthinkingly, she reached out to cover his hand with her own. 'No, of course it doesn't' she said softly. 'Look, I'm sorry. I shouldn't have said anything. . .' She shivered in spite of the heat burning in her cheeks as she became aware, yet again, of the depths of emotions of which Neil was capable.

But what about her own feelings? Where did they figure in all this? Where was it all leading? Neil wasn't a separate entity. There was Jamie, too. Jamie, who rightly deserved to be loved. Was that how Neil saw her? The thought struck her now. Was he, even without realising it, looking for a surrogate mother for his son?

The thought filled her with a sudden sense of panic. Her own experiences as a child didn't seem to offer any guidelines on that sort of thing. How would she relate to someone else's baby? Feelings could change. The Maitlands, even without being aware of it, had changed. Yes, they had loved her, in their own way. But never in quite the same way they had loved Michael.

What if she had a child of her own? Would history repeat itself? She thought about Becky. Maternal instinct was a powerful thing. It had to be, of necessity. Fond as she was of Jamie, would she be able to relate to him in the same way? For all their sakes, could she afford to take that risk?

She stirred restlessly. Neil's arm brushed against her, setting her heart racing from the brief contact. Or was it the effects of the wine? Either way it was a dangerous combination.

'It's getting late,' she said hoarsely. 'I'd better go.'

'Beth, wait.' He forestalled her attempt to open the car door as he reached towards her. She tried to move away, but his hands were on her shoulders. His dark, expensively tailored jacket brushed softly against her skin.

'Don't go.' His voice was uneven as he reached up to rake his fingers gently through her hair. 'Stay.'

'Please, don't,' she protested weakly.

In a quick, disjointed movement she pushed the door open and climbed out. But even as she fumbled for her keys he was beside her, leaning forward to cup her face in his hands and urgently drawing her towards him.

'Don't run away from me, Beth. Have you any idea of the effect you have on me?'

How could she not know? She felt the breath snag in her throat as his hands gently cupped her face, so that her nostrils were invaded by the musky, male scent of him. The warmth of his body permeated her clothes, making her all too aware of his arousal.

'I didn't imagine I'd feel this way about anyone ever again,' he breathed. His sensuous mouth was just a breath away. 'Trust me, Beth.'

Of course she trusted him. It was herself she wasn't too sure about.

His gaze narrowed. She heard his soft intake of breath as he moved closer. Her eyes closed as he bent his head slowly to brush his lips against her mouth, bringing with it a whole new kind of awareness.

She stood, stunned by the power of the sensations that coursed through her. His breath fanned her throat as he stared down at her. Her head went back as his fingers sought and found the fullness of her breast.

'I need you, Beth,' he groaned against her hair, the deepening kiss arousing her to a state of longing she had never experienced before, not even with James. *Need, want.* But needing wasn't loving, a tiny inner voice rose to taunt her.

But it was the next best thing. The thought permeated her brain. And, anyway—the thought hit her like a wave—it was already too late. She was in love with Neil Quinn.

She gasped at the shaft of exquisite pleasure his touch sent through her. This was crazy. She should put a stop to it now while there was still time.

'Neil, no!' She dragged her mouth away from the exquisite torment he was inflicting. Her senses felt drugged. She wasn't even aware of her fingers having made contact with the warm, silky smoothness of his skin beneath his shirt until she tried to draw away.

'Beth. . .'

Her head was spinning as she tried to draw away. 'Neil, don't you see? I'm not Louise. I can't *be* Louise for you.'

He relaxed his grip. 'You think I don't know that?' he said thickly.

She shook her head, pushing weakly against him. 'I know what she meant to you. I know how you must miss her,' she said bleakly. 'I understand. But don't you see? Right now neither of us is thinking rationally.'

She felt him tense. He stared at her, a nerve pulsing in his jaw, then abruptly he let her go.

'You're right. I'd hate to do something we might both regret in the cold light of day,' he rasped.

She stared at him, blinking away the tears that threatened to fall. Her fingers fumbled at the strap of her dress as she stepped away from him and, without looking back, let herself into the cottage.

It was several minutes before she heard him drive away. Only then was she able to move jerkily from the door, freeing her paralysed limbs as she headed for the bedroom to fling herself, sobbing, onto the bed.

CHAPTER SEVEN

IT CAME almost as a relief in the week that followed not to have time even to think about Neil. An outbreak of chickenpox had emptied the schools and filled the surgery. A threatened flu epidemic saw the more elderly patients queuing for vaccinations, and as a spell of particularly cold weather seemed set to continue Beth found herself facing real concern about her more vulnerable patients.

At least there was something to be said for afternoon surgery, she thought as, having parked her car, she sidestepped a puddle and headed for Reception. A morning spent spring-cleaning hadn't done much for Henry's composure, but it had certainly gone some way to lifting the vague cloud of depression which seemed to have been hanging over her for the past few days.

She walked into the office, smiling as she unfastened her jacket. 'Afternoon, Ruth.'

'Hi. You're nice and early. Probably just as well. It's already pretty full out there, I'm afraid.' Ruth nodded in the direction of the waiting room.

She handed Beth the mail, which had already been sorted, and Beth flicked through it ruefully, recognising the inevitable promotions from various drug manufacturers detailing the very latest in new products and medical care.

'Oh, well, it looks as if I won't be short of reading material for a while.' She smiled resignedly.

'There's a rep waiting to see you as well.' Ruth

handed her a business card. 'He's been waiting about half an hour. Would you like to see him now?'

Frowning, Beth looked at her watch and shook her head. 'There isn't time. Can you ask him if it's just some follow-up material on something we discussed at his last visit? If it is, perhaps you could deal with it. If it's something that needs my undivided attention, will you ask him either to hang on and see me at the end of surgery, if he can manage it, or to arrange a specific appointment for another day?'

'Will do.' Ruth nodded briskly, and reached for the telephone as it rang, leaving Beth to head along the corridor.

The door to Alex's consulting room was open and he was seated at his desk, his jacket draped over the back of the chair.

'Hi. How are you feeling now?'

He looked up with a smile as she tapped at the door. 'Much better, thanks.'

'You didn't have to rush back, you know. We were coping—just about.'

He reached for a cooling cup of coffee, draining the dregs. 'The trouble with staying at home is that it's fine for the first few days when you feel like death and want nothing more than to sleep. After that it all starts to go rapidly downhill.' He grinned. 'When I found myself sitting in front of the television, watching soaps, I knew it was time to get back to work.'

'I know what you mean.' She grinned. 'Well, as long as you're all right. . . I'd better get started or we'll have a mutiny on our hands. I'll probably see you later.'

Two minutes later she rang the bell for her first patient.

The door opened slowly and, looking up from the case notes she had quickly scanned, she watched with amusement as an elderly figure, muffled in coat, scarf and cap, edged his way round the door and regarded her suspiciously.

'Mr Hodges, do come in and tell me what I can do for you.' A quick glance at the card had showed that the patient had a history of chronic bronchitis. She indicated the chair with a smile. Sam Hodges, however, remained firmly at the door from where he grunted unhappily.

'I come to see Dr Scott. Don't hold with no female lady doctors. Ain't proper.'

Beth hid a smile. 'I'm sorry about that, Mr Hodges. Unfortunately, Dr Scott has left the practice for family reasons. Perhaps I can help, if you'd like to tell me what the problem is.'

'I been under Dr Scott. 'E knows all about me bronchials.' He coughed wheezily, and Beth felt her heart sink. It was becoming rarer these days, but there was still the occasional, usually elderly patient who felt that women had no place in medicine other than as nurses.

She smiled what she hoped was a reassuring smile. 'I'm sorry Dr Scott isn't here, but I do have his notes and I'd like to help if I can.'

Sam Hodges, a man in his mid-seventies, grunted unhappily, but ventured further into the room. 'Don't 'old with all this choppin' and changin',' he complained. 'Ain't right.'

'No, you're right. It is upsetting, but I would like to help if I can.'

He sucked at his teeth and wheezed noisily. 'Never 'eld with lady doctors. Told Bob Scott, but 'e couldn't see it. Said you 'ave to move with the times. I told 'im I 'ad my time and what weren't proper then ain't proper now. Women got their place and it ain't messin' about with men's bodies.'

Beth felt her lips quiver as he eased himself into the chair and sighed a rattling sigh. He leaned forward to tap the card in front of her.

'I'll 'ave a bottle of the usual and some of them tablets.'

Beth studied the notes and referred to her computer screen, trying to hide her confusion. The medication last prescribed was one she recognised as having proved to be most beneficial in cases like Sam Hodges, where the aim was to offer relief rather than a cure.

'I'll just have a listen to your chest, Mr Hodges.' Reaching for her stethoscope, she carried out a careful examination which only confirmed what she could see with her own eyes.

She looked at the heavily nicotine-stained fingers and said nothing. At Sam Hodges's age there was nothing to be gained by trying to persuade him to change the habit of a lifetime. Instead, having questioned him gently, she returned to her desk and printed out a prescription.

'There we are, Mr Hodges. A bottle of the usual. But I'd like you to come back and see me in about a week's time. You can make an appointment at the desk as you go out. Or you can arrange to see Dr Thornton or Dr Quinn,' she added hastily.

He got to his feet, thrust the paper carelessly into a pocket and trundled out.

Beth gave a wry smile and followed him to the door. She was about to turn away and close it when Neil appeared in the corridor. He was also seeing a patient out. He looked tired. His mouth was taut, his blue eyes hard. Beth looked at him sharply. It was almost a week since she had seen him close to, and the change in him shocked her.

On the point of closing the door, she hesitated. She

felt she should say something, but what? The distance that had opened up between them since that last meeting was like a huge void, and the pain she felt because of it was almost tangible.

She had told herself she could get over it. By throwing herself into her work, she had hoped she wouldn't have time to think. But it hadn't worked that way, not when each night she had fallen, exhausted, into bed—only to lie awake, going over and over what had happened and feeling the doubts come rushing in. The future, which only a short time ago had seemed so clear-cut, was suddenly filled with confusion. Until she had sorted out her own thoughts maybe things were best left as they were.

She gave him a remote smile and turned away.

'Beth, we need to talk.'

She paused in the doorway, looking at him. Her emotions were so close to the surface that she wasn't sure she could trust herself to be near him without letting go.

'How's Jamie?'

He frowned, dragging a hand through his hair. 'He's fine. Well, I'm not sure. He's a bit snuffly and cross. I wondered if he might be going in for this wretched chickenpox.'

So that was it. He was concerned because Jamie had a cold. She said evenly, 'You could be right. Children are often fretful when they're going down with something.'

He frowned again. 'It's times like this when I think he misses his mother. He gets clingy and reverts to his baby ways.'

She saw the expression that narrowed his eyes and etched a line into the smoothness of his brow, and guessed that he must be thinking about when Jamie had been a baby. When Louise had been there to offer comfort.

Shakily she reached out to hold onto the doorhandle. With an effort she managed to smile. 'Yes, well, I expect you'll know one way or the other in a few days. It's rotten, but he'll be fine.' She had half turned away again when he stopped her.

'Beth, I meant it.' His voice was taut. 'We do have to talk. We can't just leave things as they are.'

She looked at him and swallowed hard. 'No.' But what was there to say? The fact that she loved him didn't mean she was prepared to step into someone else's shoes. What about her own feelings? Her own needs? There were too many unanswered questions. She had half moved towards him but almost collided with Emma, who was hovering in the corridor.

'Sorry to interrupt, but there are some more cards. Last-minute arrivals, I'm afraid.' She handed them to Beth and looked at Neil. 'And there's a phone call for you, Dr Quinn. Wadeley General. The results of some tests you wanted urgently.'

He looked at his watch, his dark brows drawing together. 'Damn! Look, you'd better put it through.' He glanced at Beth. 'I meant what I said. Perhaps we can get together later?'

'Fine.' With an effort, she managed a smile and felt her heart contract with misery as she watched his door close. But some things no amount of talking could solve, she thought as she returned to her own room and waited for her next patient—a young woman with a small child who looked decidedly feverish and was crying lethargically.

Beth questioned the mother, whilst making a gentle but thorough examination of the child who was three years old.

'I can't understand it, Doctor. Natalie's not a child who cries for nothing. She's bright, and when she says she's got a headache I know she means it.'

Beth nodded, frowning. 'Yes, I can see she has, and quite a nasty one, too, by the look of her.' She took a fever-strip from the drawer and pressed it to the child's forehead. The temperature was definitely raised, but there was no evidence of a sore throat. 'Has she complained of a tummyache?'

'No.' The mother frowned. 'But, actually, she has been sick, and she seems to keep bumping into things, as if she's giddy. You know what I mean? One minute she's right as rain and next she's like this.'

'Ah.' Beth smiled as she drew the child towards her so that she was leaning comfortably against her knee. 'Let's take a quick look in your ears, shall we, Natalie? See if we can find out what's going on in there. Has she had a cold, Mrs Taylor?'

The woman considered. 'Well, yes, now that you mention it. A couple of weeks ago. Quite a heavy one, but she seemed to be over it.'

Beth made a gentle examination of the child's ears and listened to her chest, confirming the suspicion which had gradually begun to form in her mind.

Guiding the child back to her mother, she tapped out a prescription. 'I'm going to give you an antihistamine for Natalie, Mrs Taylor. You'll find it should help control the nausea and the balance problem. In fact, the two are connected. It's a bit like sea-sickness.'

'But. . .what is it, Doctor?'

'Natalie has a condition called labyrinthitis.'

'Labyrinthitis? I've never heard of it.'

'No, it's not terribly common in children as young as Natalie. What's happened is that her ears have been affected by the heavy cold, and because of that her balance is affected and that causes her to feel sick. But, as I say, this medicine should help. I'll give her an antibiotic, too, because her chest is still quite rattly.

'Hopefully, you'll see a fairly rapid improvement in the next few days. She may be a bit drowsy, but sleep is probably the best thing for her at the moment. You will make sure she completes the course of antibiotics, won't you?'

'I will, Doctor.' Janice Taylor got to her feet, clutching the prescription.

'You'd be surprised how many people stop taking the medication when they start to feel better,' Beth said.

'It'll be a relief to have her back to normal again. I know I complain when she's noisy but I'd rather have her like that than this.'

It was a cry echoed by so many mothers that Beth smiled. She had just seen the last of her patients out and was looking forward to a cup of coffee when someone tapped at the door and came in.

'Not more?' she groaned.

'Sorry.' Ruth gave a rueful smile as she put a cup of coffee on the desk. 'A call just came in from Mrs Warner, over at Stokeley.'

'Warner?' Beth frowned.

'She sounds pretty worried. She and her husband used to be Bob Scott's patients, then transferred to Neil's list. But he's just left. He had a couple of calls. . .'

'It's all right, I'll take it.' Beth was already on her feet, reaching for her coat and the piece of paper. 'What's the problem, do we know?'

Ruth shook her head. 'She wasn't exactly coherent. I know the Warners are both in their late seventies. She says her husband has collapsed. I tried to get her to be more specific, but she was worried and wanted to get back to him. She put the phone down.'

'I'd better get over there.' Reaching for her briefcase, Beth gulped the scalding black coffee before she headed for the door. 'Is Neil coming back to the surgery later, do you know?'

'Not as far as I know. He wanted to get back to Jamie, and Alex is on duty call.'

Beth nodded and hurried out to her car, gasping as a wave of cold air hit her. It was already dark and the road was icy. It needed all her powers of concentration to keep the car steady.

Ten minutes later she pulled up and looked at the small terraced house where lights were blazing. Reaching for her briefcase, she briefly had time to notice that the sky was clear and full of stars before the door opened and a figure drew her anxiously into the house.

'Oh, Doctor, I'm so glad you've come. I didn't know what to do. I can't move him.'

Beth gently ushered the woman inside. 'Where is your husband, Mrs Warner? Upstairs?'

'No.' Audrey Warner's lips quivered. 'He's through here.' She led the way through to the kitchen. 'That's it, you see? He said he'd just make a cup of tea while I was watching television. He's very good like that is Ted.'

Beth walked into the kitchen, took one look at the man lying on the floor and went quickly towards him, setting her briefcase down beside her. His face was pale and dotted with perspiration and there was a greyish-blue tinge to his lips. Her fingers felt rapidly for a pulse.

'It's a heart attack, isn't it?' Tears flooded into Audrey Warner's eyes as Beth nodded.

'It looks very much like it, I'm afraid, though at this stage it's difficult to tell how serious it is. It's all right, Mr Warner. I know you're not feeling well. I'm just going to give you an injection to ease the pain. No. . .

don't try to move. Just relax.' She smiled. 'Let everyone else do the work for a change.'

Audrey Warner clutched at her throat. 'I wouldn't have known. He could have been there for half an hour or more if he hadn't dropped the biscuit tin as he fell. He often comes in here to read the paper, you see. I heard the crash—'

'Had he complained earlier of feeling unwell?'

'Well, he. . .he said he had a touch of indigestion. I thought it was after the fish we had for tea. Ted likes a bit of fish, even though it doesn't always agree with him, so I didn't think too much of it when he said he was going to take a couple of tablets.'

'I take it he didn't get any better?'

'No. In fact, he started getting very fidgety and cross, and I said if he didn't get any better I was going to call the surgery. And then. . .'

Beth was on her feet, scarcely hearing what the distraught woman was saying. She reached for her mobile phone, tapping out a number.

'I'm calling for an ambulance, Mrs Warner. Hopefully, it should only take a few minutes. In the meantime, I've given your husband an injection which should make him feel a little more comfortable. Perhaps you'd like to pack a few of his things into a bag.'

'I want to go with him, Doctor. I'm not leaving him.'

'Yes, of course.' Beth nodded gently. 'That won't be a problem.' She scanned the small figure. 'If you'd like to get a coat I expect the ambulance will be here soon.'

'He's. . .he's going to be all right, isn't he, doctor?'

Beth held the woman's hand. 'You did the right thing, calling as quickly as you did. He'll soon be in hospital where they'll take good care of him.' Beth knew from long experience never to raise false hopes in either a patient or the family.

A short time later the ambulance arrived with its blue light flashing but it was still going to be a long struggle for Ted Warner. Half an hour later, having seen the ambulance bear the patient away, Beth was on her way back to the cottage.

By now it was well into the evening. She felt physically tired and emotionally exhausted yet, frustratingly, she felt too keyed up, too depressed, thinking of the elderly couple, to be able to contemplate eating a meal and climbing into bed for the early night she had promised herself.

Sighing heavily, she realised that Neil would have to be told what had happened. The Warners were his patients. He would want to know.

Automatically she slowed the car and reached for the mobile phone, only to tense her fingers round it. This is ridiculous, she thought. What are you so afraid of? It made no sense to phone when she had to drive past the house.

She brought the car to a halt and switched off the engine but made no attempt to move, staring into the darkness instead. The lights were on in Neil's house. Her hands clenched against the wheel. He was right. Sooner or later they had to talk. Too much had been left unsaid, and the more she tried to face the possibility of a future without him the more she knew she didn't want it to happen.

With a sigh of exasperation, she reached for her jacket and briefcase and got out of the car. Standing outside Neil's door, she raised her hand, hesitated for a second and then rang the bell.

For a moment a feeling of relief swept over her as no one answered. Perhaps he was out and had left the lights on purposely as a security measure. She had already half turned away when the door opened, letting out a flood of light, and he was standing there with a tea towel in one hand and a look of surprise on his face while she stood rooted to the spot.

She swallowed hard. 'I'm sorry, I know it's late and you're off duty. . .'

He paused, then stepped back into the hall. 'You'd better come in.'

She hesitated. 'I don't want to intrude. . .'

'You're not intruding.' Frowning, he glanced at the teatowel. 'I was just trying to restore some kind of order. It beats me how cooking a few fish fingers and opening a can of spaghetti can get out of hand. We're through here.'

She followed him into the kitchen where Jamie, in pyjamas, was sitting at the table, drinking a glass of milk and colouring pictures in a large book.
His hair was still damp, as if he had just had a bath.

'Jamie, look who's here. Beth's come to see you.'

Blue eyes beamed at her over the glass, a milky white moustache outlining his mouth as he pronounced gleefully, 'I was sick.'

She grinned. 'You certainly were. How are the twins?'

'Thomas fell off his bike and hurt his knee. It bleeded.'

With an effort, she kept her face serious. 'Oh, no! Is he all right?'

He nodded, concentrating as he swirled bright red colour onto the page. 'Auntie Sally put a plaster on it. I've got one, too.' He held up one chubby hand, sporting a large plaster. 'Daddy kissed it better.'

Suddenly her heart gave an odd little lurch. She wanted to run and pick him up, kiss the bright little button nose and nuzzle the chubby, warm, baby softness of his cheeks and neck.

It would be so easy to love him, this other woman's child. If she was honest, she was already more than halfway to loving him. Her throat tightened in a painful spasm. But what about when she held her own child in her arms? Even without knowing it and without wishing it, she might love it more because it was what Jamie could never be—her own flesh and blood. Was it a risk she dared take?

She looked up, her gaze locking intently with Neil's, and she saw his mouth twitch.

'Paul's got one, too. They're trying for the sympathy vote. At this rate I may run out of plasters. Coffee?'

'Well, I—'

'It's fresh.'

'In that case. . .' She set her briefcase down.

'Pop your jacket over the chair.'

She hadn't intended to stay but somehow he was doing it again, taking charge, and she was going along with it. Before she knew what was happening she was ensconced at the table with a mug of coffee in front of her, and Jamie had edged his way into the seat beside her, bringing his colouring book and paints with him. He smelled of talcum powder.

'I painted at school.'

'You're very good at it, aren't you?'

He leaned his chin on one pudgy hand, plying blue paint enthusiastically with the other. 'Daddy drawed me a nelephant wiv long ears.'

'Did he really?' In spite of herself, Beth grinned. 'Clever Daddy.'

The paintbrush plopped into a jar of water. 'Daddy, I finished.' Rivulets of paint dripped onto the table. 'I did it all by myself.'

Beth watched in rapt fascination as Neil took the sodden page, gazing in studied admiration at merging pools of blue, red and yellow. 'Well, I think that's brilliant.'

'You really like it?' Blue, heavily lashed eyes, so like his own, beamed with delight, and Beth felt as if someone had reached out and tugged at her heart.

'I really do. In fact, it's so good I think we should let it dry and then we'll put it on the wall. What do you think?'

'Yeah!'

Beth grinned. 'A budding Picasso, no less.'

Neil made a slight sound in his throat. 'You should see the others. I'm rapidly running out of wall space.'

She grinned. 'I'm all for encouraging artistic talent.'

'Well, thanks a bunch. I can always arrange for you to take delivery of the odd dozen or so,' he shot back with an easy familiarity that did something to her heart.

'I can paint a nuvver one, wiv a train on.' The brush was already swirling in the jar again as Jamie yawned widely.

Neil ruffled his son's hair. 'It's getting a bit late now, tiger. How about finishing your milk, then I'll pop you up to bed? Are you going to say goodnight to Beth?'

Jamie scanned her face and then, with a grin, flung his arms round her neck, planting a prolonged kiss firmly on her cheek. 'Night, Beff.'

She hugged him. 'Sleep tight, poppet.'

He yawned again, rescued a teddy from under his chair and headed for the door. 'Come on, Daddy.'

'I'm right with you. Brush your teeth.' Neil paused in the doorway. 'There's more coffee, if you want it. I'll be five minutes.' He smiled wryly. 'This is getting to be a habit.'

A habit she could get to like. 'I'll be fine.' She swallowed hard. 'Go and see to Jamie.'

Left to her own devices, she wandered through to the sitting room. Listening to the sounds coming from upstairs, she took advantage of the moments alone to study the room, her eye caught by the details—subtle changes he had made, even in so short a time. Changes which stamped his own personality upon it—a lamp reflecting in polished surfaces, the dark wood furniture, pictures on the walls. Bookshelves, a box of toys in the corner. Already there was a settled feel about it. A kind of permanence.

She sat in one of the large armchairs. There was something almost hypnotic about a real fire, watching the flames, orange, red and blue, lick around the logs. Already this was more than a house. It was a home, warm and filled with the kind of love that was almost tangible. The kind of home he had once shared with Louise?

'I'll be with you in a minute,' Neil called from the kitchen. 'Why don't you pour yourself a proper drink?'

'I'm driving, don't forget.' She raised her voice to remind him.

'Orange juice, then.'

She looked up to see him standing in the doorway. He was studying her so intently that she rose quickly. 'I'm sorry, I made myself a little too comfortable.' She ran a hand awkwardly through her hair.

'Don't apologise,' he said huskily. 'I was just thinking I might join you. Have you eaten?'

'What?'

'Eaten—as in food, sustenance?'

She shook her head, frowning. 'I don't seem to have had time.'

'I thought not. I've got a couple of steaks in the fridge and I can rustle up a salad.'

'Look, really, you don't have to—'

'I haven't eaten, anyway, and it's just as easy to cook for two as one. Besides, everything's under control.'

Except my heart, she thought wildly. There was something disturbingly arousing about him as he stood with the light from the lamp behind him, his faded jeans hugging his hips and his eyes appearing a deeper blue than ever.

She let her gaze fall warily. 'The reason I came was to let you know that I've admitted one of your patients to hospital.'

'Who?'

'Ted Warner.'

'Warner?' He frowned. 'Oh, yes, I remember. He and his wife live over in Stokeley. An elderly couple.'

She nodded. 'I'm afraid he's had a heart attack.'

'Oh, God. How bad is it?'

'Not good,' she said flatly. 'His wife is pretty devastated. I've arranged for her to stay at the hospital with him for as long as she needs to. At least he's in the best possible hands.'

Neil sighed. 'They're a nice couple. I'll call the hospital later to see how he's doing. Look, I'm grateful—'

'There's no need.' She gave a slight laugh. 'Actually, I feel guilty.'

'For heaven's sake, why?'

'I come bearing bad news and get fed for my pains.'

'It's the least I can do,' he said softly. 'I really am grateful.' He leaned forward, pulling her gently towards him, and she could smell the subtle, musky tones of his aftershave.

The effect of his nearness was creating an intensity

of sexual awareness. She must have been crazy to think she could remain indifferent. There were problems enough in any relationship, but she must be mad to think even about getting involved with a man who was still in love with his wife. He had a child, too. A dear, sweet boy, but another woman's child.

'God, if you knew how much I've wanted to do this.'

'Neil, I don't think this is a good idea,' she murmured, tilting her head back to look at him.

She fought a rising sense of panic. This wasn't supposed to be happening. She had told herself it wouldn't, but suddenly resistance was a word that seemed to have been removed from her vocabulary as very gently his palm slid round her waist, drawing her closer.

'Don't you see?' she said weakly. 'Nothing's changed.'

He tensed briefly, looking down at her. 'You mean Louise?' Frowning, he ran his fingers through her hair. 'Beth, Louise is gone. I can't tell you I'll ever forget her. I did love her, I always will.' He felt her hands tense. 'But that doesn't mean I'm not allowed a second chance, that I can't fall in love again.'

'You know what you're saying?' She trembled, vaguely aware of the lingering trace of aftershave and the fact that, almost imperceptibly, he had drawn her closer.

'Beth, I love you.' He saw her eyes widen. 'It has nothing to do with my feelings for Louise. What I felt then is not the same as now. *You're* part of my life now. I need you. Jamie needs you.'

His mouth was warm and persuasive and she was helpless to prevent the faint quivering of her lips beneath his as she fought the steady increase of tension, the building of desire as it washed over her and threatened to drown her beneath its onslaught.

'We can work things out,' he rasped.

He made it sound so easy. She wanted to be convinced. It would be so easy to give in and to let it happen.

She shook her head in confusion. 'I don't know, Neil. . .' She was trembling as she tried to pull away from him and think clearly.

You don't have to be afraid,' he said raggedly. 'I've no intention of rushing things, Beth, however much I might be tempted.'

So why did she feel she was sliding down a slope, totally out of control?

His blue eyes searched her face intently as he touched her cheek. 'I wouldn't do anything to hurt you. Trust me, Beth.'

She was torn. She did trust him, but was he thinking logically? Maybe he was trying to fill a void, to look to the future. If only he wouldn't hold her this way, undermining all her resolve. Too many people stood to get hurt if she made the wrong decision.

A nerve pulsed in his jaw as he drew her towards him. 'I want you, Beth.' He groaned softly as his mouth made teasing advances against her lips, her throat, his tautly muscled body so close that she could feel the thud of his heart. The effect was devastating, and suddenly she was responding with a ferocity that matched his own, driven by a raw kind of hunger.

'Beth, oh, Beth.' He spoke softly as she opened her eyes to find his deep blue gaze on her.

It was unfair, she thought as he kissed her again. She felt as if she were walking on quicksand. She gasped at the shaft of pleasure his touch sent thrilling through her. Loving Neil wasn't at issue. It was her own doubts she had to face and somehow overcome.

Until now, she realised with a sudden sense of shock,

she had been too busy—with her studies, then with her medical training—even to think about the future. It hadn't seemed important.

Now, suddenly, everything had changed. Barriers she had never even known existed were suddenly looming up in front of her. Questions—about love, marriage and the family—needed answers, and all she had to draw on were her own experiences. Suddenly they seemed to be confused and totally inadequate.

She *did* love Neil. That was the one thing she was absolutely sure of now. But how could she give him the kind of commitment he wanted—deserved? How could she be a mother to his child when she hadn't known her own mother?

She closed her eyes, moaning softly as the whole gamut of emotions ran through her.

'I love you, Beth.'

'I know,' she sighed fretfully. 'I want you, too. I. . .I love you, too.'

He drew a harsh breath as he looked at her for a long moment, then pulled her roughly towards him. 'Stay with me tonight.'

Desire licked like a flame at her senses, sending dangerous signals to her brain. Crazy, crazy. But her fingers ran over the strong column of his neck, tangling in the dark silkiness of his nape.

'We should talk,' she breathed. 'You don't know—'

'We can talk later.' His hand brushed against her cheek.

'I'm still on call,' she protested weakly. 'And what about Jamie?' Yes, what about Jamie? The voice of her conscience homed in with deadly accuracy.

'He's asleep.'

She rocked on her feet. Her senses seemed drugged

as she looked up at him. 'You make it all sound so simple.'

'Because it *is* simple,' he said huskily. His fingers had long since dealt with the buttons on her blouse.

It was so unfair. If he kissed her again—

The mobile phone rang. She gasped disbelievingly.

'Ignore it,' he rasped. His lips drew her own back, but with the strident sound common sense returned rapidly and she pushed him gently away, trying to steady her breathing.

'You know I can't. It might be urgent.' She groped behind her for the phone, fumbling for the button as Neil's face followed her own until she deliberately tilted her head out of his reach and said breathlessly, 'Yes, Dr Maitland speaking.'

Neil murmured wickedly against her ear, 'No need to be so formal, darling.'

In desperation she pushed him away. He wasn't making this easy.

'Yes, and he has abdominal pains? Has he been sick? Right, I'll be there in about fifteen minutes.' She ended the call and took a deep breath. Her cheeks felt flushed and she could only imagine how she must look. 'It sounds as if it may be appendicitis. I have to go, Neil.'

'I know.' He followed her slowly to the door and helped her into her jacket, his hands tightening on her shoulders. He bent his head to kiss her. 'Drive carefully.'

'I will.' She looked up at him, shivering in the freezing night air. 'I really am sorry—'

'Don't be,' he said. Slowly he let her go. 'I'll see you in the morning,' he breathed, leaving her with the feeling that she hadn't won the battle, merely postponed the war!

CHAPTER EIGHT

ALTHOUGH she hadn't expected to, Beth fell into a deep sleep almost the instant her head touched the pillow. Exhaustion and nervous tension had finally set in so that, for the first time in weeks, she slept soundly. So soundly, in fact, that it took several minutes for the loud shrilling of the phone to penetrate her sleep-fogged brain.

Groaning into her pillow, she opened one eye to stare disbelievingly at the clock. *Five-thirty a.m!* She felt shaky and drugged as she reached out a hand, fumbled for the bedside lamp, then the receiver and said huskily, 'Dr Maitland.'

Minutes later she was heading for the bathroom, struggling into her clothes as she gulped at a strong, black coffee to wake her up. Her bag was beside her coat. Barely flicking a comb through her hair, she went out to the car and gasped as the dawn chill hit her.

As she drove she stifled a yawn. The road was icy and it needed all her powers of concentration to keep the car steady. The Ingrams were a couple in their mid-thirties, new to the area. She vaguely remembered seeing Dawn Ingrams at the surgery.

As she approached the door of the neat, modern house the door opened and a figure came out to meet her.

'Sorry to call you out at this hour of the morning, Doctor,' Keith Ingrams kept insisting as he ushered Beth into the sitting room. 'I wanted to ring you a couple of hours ago, but Dawn wouldn't have it. I'm really worried about her, Doctor.'

'Don't worry about it.' Beth smiled as she put her bag down before she moved to the sofa, where a heavily pregnant young woman sat, with her eyes closed and her head resting against the back. One hand was clasped to her stomach as she breathed deeply. 'So, what's the problem?' Automatically her fingers went to the woman's wrist, searching for the pulse.

'She's been getting pains for about two hours now.' Looking agitated, Keith Ingrams sat in the chair opposite. 'And they're getting stronger.'

'I keep telling him he's fussing for nothing.' His wife's face contorted. 'It's wind, that's all. I made a rhubarb pie last night.'

'Well, you could be right, then,' said Beth. 'It has been known to have that effect. How often are you getting the pains? Or are they there all the time?' She pressed a hand gently to the woman's abdomen, feeling the gathering strength of a contraction.

'About. . .every ten minutes,' came the grunted response. 'Serves me right for having a second helping.' Her laughter was strained as she struggled unsteadily to her feet, leaning against the chair with one hand.

'And when is the baby actually due? You must be getting quite excited.'

'Next month.' Keith Ingrams was on his feet again, anxiously watching his wife.

'Not for another five weeks.' She pressed a hand to her back. 'As for excited, it's not the word I'd have used, Doctor. Bored is more like it, and this last couple of weeks have been the worst. I can't sleep. I reckon this baby is going to be born wearing his dad's football boots.' She leaned forward, sucking in a breath. 'Its feet are everywhere.' She bit at her lip. 'It's no wonder I've got backache.'

Warning bells were clanging loud and clear in Beth's head. Glancing at the window, she saw that it was snowing heavily again. 'Have you been coming to the surgery regularly for your ante-natal check-ups? Only I usually see most of the expectant mums. . .'

Colour briefly flooded the woman's face. 'I meant to come. I know I should have. But you know how it is.' She eased herself carefully into the chair again. 'What with work, and we've been doing up the house. Well, there's never the time somehow.'

'Yes, I know it can be a bit of a bind.' Now was hardly the time for a lecture. 'Look, are you absolutely sure about your dates?'

'Yes.' The couple looked at each other and Keith Ingrams grinned sheepishly. 'We'd been on holiday, you see. We'd often talked about having a baby, but we wanted to wait till we'd got the house and. . .well, somehow the time seemed right. So we're pretty sure.' His grin faded. 'It is going to be all right, isn't it, Doctor?'

Beth nodded, smiling what she hoped was a reassuring smile. If Dawn Ingrams's dates *were* right this baby was arriving prematurely, and it was pretty clear from what she'd said that she hadn't bothered to have regular ante-natal check-ups.

She turned just in time to see Dawn sit upright in the chair, her eyes closed and her hands gripping the chair arms. Beth reached for her sphygmomanometer, her suspicions confirmed as the woman opened her eyes again, exhaling deeply.

'It *is* the baby, isn't it?' Her grip relaxed gradually as the contraction subsided. 'But it's too soon. Perhaps it's a false alarm.'

'It could be, but I think I'd better check you over just in case,' Beth said briskly. 'Babies have an annoying habit of not always sticking to dates.'

'But. . .' There was a look of panic in the woman's eyes now. 'Is it going to be all right?' She reached out to clutch at her husband's hand. 'There should be another five or six weeks to go.'

'I'm sure it will be. As I said, it's possible you may have your dates wrong. The baby looks to be a pretty good size.' A swift examination soon confirmed that this baby was definitely in something of a hurry to be born.

As Beth scrubbed her hands Dawn Ingrams breathed deeply through another contraction and Beth glanced at her watch. 'Well, you're definitely in labour. The best thing we can do is get you some help. Where are you booked to have the baby?'

'At the maternity unit in Wadeley. But I don't think I'm going. . .to make it.' Her hands gripped the chair again.

Beth reached for her mobile phone. 'Try to relax.' She smiled. 'I know it's not easy but it really will help. I'm going to ring for an ambulance. They'll have someone here in no time.'

She was already tapping out the number of the local maternity unit, but when was answered the sister's voice was brisk and apologetic.

'We'll do out best, Doctor, but we've had a rush on, and the weather's not helping. The drivers are doing their best but the roads are bad. Just hang on. We'll try to get someone to you as soon as we can.'

Beth smiled ruefully. 'I will, Sister, though I'm not sure I can say the same for Mrs Ingrams.'

Minutes later, having dispatched the anxious father-to-be to the kitchen to make tea, she was helping his wife up the stairs and into bed.

'I'll just pop down and get my briefcase.' Beth had just shed her jacket, rolled up her sleeves and was on her way back up the stairs when Dawn Ingrams's voice called waveringly.

'D—Doctor. Oh. . .something's happening.'

Beth's feet flew. Her movements were purely instinctive as she prayed that everything was going to be straight forward and that the ambulance would arrive within the next few minutes.

In the event, a flushed Keith Ingrams answered the door. The ambulance driver and his partner ran up the stairs, knocking at the door just as Beth was wrapping a sturdy, red-faced infant in a towel and placing him in his mother's arms.

Terry Barnes grinned. 'Looks as if we left it a bit late, but you seem have managed very nicely without us, Doctor.'

Beth looked at the exhausted but happy young woman in the bed and pronounced, as a grinning husband rushed through the door, 'Congratulations, Mr Ingrams, you have a perfectly healthy, seven-and-a-half-pound little footballer. He and his mum are doing nicely.'

Half an hour later, having scrubbed her hands, she picked up her briefcase and eyed the happy group. 'Well, there's nothing more I can do here for now. Everything was perfectly straightforward. The midwife will be in to see you later.'

'Doctor,' Dawn Ingrams called as she reached the door. 'Thanks for everything. I don't know what we'd have done if you hadn't been here.'

'I'm sure you'd have managed. But just don't go eating any more rhubarb for a while.' Beth grinned.

'The baby won't like it. Anyway. . .' she glanced at her watch '. . .I'd better be off.'

She left them to it. A happy couple, slightly bewildered but suddenly a family. It wasn't until she was driving back along the lanes that she realised she was tired. Giving birth was an exhausting business, she decided, for everyone concerned.

Driving to the surgery as the first streaks of daylight were brightening the sky, she had time to appreciate the peace and tranquillity of a new day. The distant harbour was calm, with the rising sun cutting a golden path across the water. She slowed the car for a moment and shaded her eyes to watch a flotilla of small fishing boats head out to sea, and experienced the same delight she always had, even as a child, at the sight.

She had decided against going back to the cottage. There seemed little point in falling into bed, only to have to climb out again an hour later.

Instead, she headed for the surgery, telling herself as she sat at her desk catching up with a backlog of letters that at least there were advantages to arriving early. By the time Annie Collins, the practice nurse, popped her head round the door an hour later she was actually beginning to feel she had made some headway.

'You're an early bird. What's this, then? Couldn't you sleep or something?'

'Chance would be a fine thing.' Beth looked up, grinning. 'I got a call at five-thirty. Mrs Ingrams went into labour.'

'Ingrams?' Annie frowned, easing herself out of her coat. 'I thought her baby wasn't due for another month or so?'

'Well. . .' Beth stifled a yawn '. . .it decided it couldn't wait. She had a boy—just before the ambulance arrived. Mum, Dad and baby are all doing well.'

She leaned back in her chair. 'By the time I finally got away it was hardly worth going back to bed. I thought I might as well come in and catch up on a few things.'

Glancing at her watch, she sighed and rose to her feet. 'And now I suppose I'd better think about surgery. What's it like out there?'

'Hectic. They were starting to queue at the desk.' Smiling and neat in her blue uniform, Annie followed her out. 'I'll pop in to see Mrs Ingrams later.'

'Give the baby a kiss from me.'

'Will do.'

'Morning. You're nice and early.' Ruth hunted through the growing mountain of paperwork on her desk. 'Morning post, patients' cards.' She handed them over. 'And. . .where is it? Ah, the results of that second smear. You remember the one?'

'At last.' Anxiously, Beth scanned the letter and gave a sigh of relief. 'It's clear. I expect Mrs Duncan will be calling in today. At least we can put her mind at rest. I know she's been worried sick.'

'I can imagine.'

'Anyway, time I made a start.'

It was a long morning, the bright spot of which turned out to be Anna Richards who had been to see the eye specialist.

'So, how did you get on?'

'He says he's really not convinced that I have glaucoma,' she announced in response to the query. 'He says the pressure in my eyes *is* up, but the results of the other tests they did weren't conclusive.'

'Well, at least that's a good sign.'

'I know. That's what I thought.'

'So what happens now?' Beth sorted through her notes. 'I don't seem to have the report through yet.'

'He wants to see me again in about three months time so that they can do another field test. You know, the one with the flashing lights.'

'How was it?'

'Fine. Nothing to worry about at all,' the woman said. 'I really don't know why I was so nervous. Anyway, he was a lovely man—very understanding. He said even if they find I do have glaucoma at least they've caught it in the very early stages. I'm so relieved, and I'm so glad I went to the optician to have my eyes tested when I did.' She gave a slight laugh.

'I certainly won't put it off again, no matter what the results are next time. And I'll make jolly sure the family get their eyes tested regularly, too.'

By the time she had seen the last patient out Beth's head was thumping and she went in search of coffee. She was just swallowing a couple of aspirins when the door opened and Neil walked in. He was wearing a dark suit and he looked tired, and it needed an effort of will on her part not to rush into his arms.

'Great minds obviously think alike.'

'Was that the coffee or the aspirins?' she said lightly.

'Both.'

She handed him a cup and watched him spoon in three sugars. 'You look awful.'

'Why, Dr Maitland, you say the nicest things.'

'We aim to please.' She swallowed the dregs of her coffee, scalding her throat in the process, and put her cup down. 'Well, I was just on my way—'

'Beth, don't go.' She turned slowly to look at him. 'How was the patient?'

'Patient?'

His mouth quirked. 'The one who needed your urgent attention.'

'Oh. It was appendicitis. I got him to hospital. Hopefully, by now he should be feeling much better.' She had to clear her throat. 'Look, I left in something of a hurry last night. I didn't get a chance to thank you for the drink. . .'

'Forget it,' he said huskily and moved closer. She found her gaze drawn to the firm line of his jaw and the blue eyes which seemed to having a strangely hypnotic effect, drawing her towards him. 'We both know it's only delaying the inevitable, don't we, Beth?'

Her pulse rate accelerated dangerously. 'I don't know what you mean.'

'Oh, I think you do,' he said softly. His glittering gaze was brooding as he drew her towards him. She looked at him and felt a sensation of pure excitement run through her, sending dangerous signals to her brain. Why couldn't everything be simple, straightforward?

'Neil, I don't think this is the right time. We can't just pick up where we left off,' she murmured breathlessly, tilting her head to look at him.

'Why not? It seems as good a place as any.' His thumb grazed her cheek. 'We never seem to have time to talk. I mean, really talk. Last night I didn't want you to go.'

'I had no choice—you know that.'

'If you had, would it have made any difference?'

She moved restlessly. 'Neil, I don't know. I'm so confused. When I'm with you. . .' why did he have to make things more difficult? She closed her eyes in a feeble and totally unsuccessful attempt to shut him out. She might have known it wouldn't work. How could it when he only had to be near her for nervous system to feel as if it were on fire?

'I meant what I said. I need you in my life, Beth. I can't let you go, just watch you walk away—you do know that?'

She felt the breath snag in her throat. 'I'm not sure what I feel or think any more, except that—'

'You can't deny that you want it, too.'

'No, I can't deny it,' she whispered. 'I just know it isn't as easy or as simple as you make it seem. . .'

'But you want me?'

'Yes,' she sighed. What was the point in denying it when her own body betrayed her as soon as he came near? A shudder of desire racked her. 'But, don't you see, we don't really know each other? There are things. . .'

'I know all I need to know,' he murmured against her cheek as he cupped her face in his hands, urgently drawing her closer. 'I have to go on with my life, Beth. I want *you* to be a part of my life. Is that so very wrong?'

There was nothing wrong with it at all. She moaned softly as his mouth fastened on hers. The sensation was electric. Beth hesitated only a moment, then her head went back as she gave herself up to the tide of emotions which was sweeping her along, taking her doubts with it.

When you loved someone surely anything was possible? Well, she did love Neil—Jamie, too. That had to count for something. Didn't they say love could conquer anything?

Beth thought about her adoptive parents and felt her throat tighten. They had always been kind, and as she had grown older she had come to the realisation that they would never knowingly have hurt her. They had simply been blinkered, so blinded by their own desperation to have a child of their own that they had become less aware of the five-year-old who had also had needs but who had been replaced in their affections by the new baby.

Her body trembled beneath the onslaught as Neil's

hands slid beneath her jacket, caressing the fullness of her breasts. She was incapable of rational thought. Her body swayed closer, restlessly seeking some elusive fulfilment.

Neil stiffened. He released her gently, and she uttered a small cry of protest. He swore softly. Only then did she also become aware that someone was tapping loudly at the door.

Beth's fingers shook as she struggled to restore her clothes to some sort of order, just as Ruth popped her head round the door.

'Sorry to disturb you, but there was a phone call for you, Beth. I tried your office. It was Mrs Dawson.' Her expression was grim and Beth stiffened involuntarily.

'Becky?'

'It's the baby,' Ruth's voice shook and Beth felt her stomach tighten. 'Someone's taken her. They've been searching for the past hour but there's no sign of her. The poor woman is absolutely distraught.'

Beth felt suddenly very cold. 'I have to go to her.' She looked vaguely at Ruth. 'My calls. . .'

'It's all right,' came the quick reassurance. 'Alex heard the news. He said he'll deal with them.'

Beth nodded mutely, moistening her dry lips with her tongue.

'I'll take you over there.' Neil was instantly at her side, his hand under her elbow.

'But your patients. . .'

'There aren't any. I'd seen the last. Besides, I have the car phone. If anyone needs me they can still reach me.' He looked at Ruth, who nodded.

Beth was vaguely aware of his hand, supporting her, as they went in silence out to his car.

As he drove she stared out of the window, willing him to go faster. 'I can't believe this is happening,' she said dully. 'I've known Becky since we were in nursery school together. I'm going to be godmother to her baby. . .'

Neil's hand reached out and closed over her own as he briefly took his eyes from the road to look at her.

'Hold on, my love. Five minutes and we'll be there.'

She nodded, turning her head to stare blankly into the fading light. 'They waited so long for this baby,' she said tautly. 'The IVF treatment was their last resort. If anything happens. . .'

'Don't, Beth,' he said softly. 'Everything's going to be all right. They'll get her back.'

'How can you be so sure? Where do you start when something like this happens? What do you do? I feel so. . .useless.'

Neil's grip tightened briefly. 'You just have to be there for her. That's a start,' he said quietly.

She passed her tongue over her lips again, very conscious of his presence beside her as the car finally came to a halt and she climbed out.

The front door opened even as she hurried towards it, and Becky, distraught and white-faced, flung herself, sobbing, into Beth's arms.

'They've taken her,' she sobbed uncontrollably. 'They've taken my baby. I've looked everywhere.' She raked a hand through her hair. 'I don't know what to do, Beth. I can't bear it. If they hurt her. . .'

Beth held her friend, tears in her own eyes as she waited for the convulsions of grief to subside. It was Neil who led them into the house, where a young policewoman emerged from the kitchen to set a tray of tea on the table.

She greeted their arrival with a look of relief. 'She asked for you,' she said quietly as Beth helped Becky into a chair. 'I understand you're Mrs Dawson's doctor.'

'And her friend.'

'Well, she certainly needs you. I'm Police Constable Jackson, by the way.' She smiled slightly. 'Call me Liz.'

'Has anyone been able to contact George? He'll be devastated.'

'We're still trying. We've been in contact with his office, but apparently he's *en route* to a meeting. They're trying to get a message to him.'

Neil came towards them. 'I've persuaded her to take a sedative. I know it won't solve the problem, or bring the baby back, but it may help her to cope. At least until the worst is over.'

'How exactly did it happen?' Beth asked.

Liz Jackson frowned. 'As far as we can make out—'

'I'd put her in the car,' Becky said quietly. She was shaking violently as she looked at them, her face ashen and tear-stained. 'It was on the drive. We were going to the shops. I put her in her car seat. . .' She closed her eyes. 'The phone rang. I know I should have ignored it, but George had forgotten some papers. I thought. . .I thought it might be him so I went to answer it. I was only gone a few seconds.'

'It's all right.' Beth put an arm round her friend's shoulders. 'It's going to be all right.'

Neil said, 'They'll find her.'

'Promise me,' came the whispered reply.

Beth met his gaze. She swallowed hard on the tightness in her throat, then she nodded. 'Whoever has her won't have got far.'

'But how do you know they'll look after her?'

'I know it probably isn't much consolation,' Neil

said gruffly, 'but in most cases like this the baby is usually well cared for.'

'But she's so tiny. She needs.me.' Becky's panic-stricken gaze flew to Beth. 'She's still poorly. She needs her medicine. How do I know they'll look after her?'

'Becky, I—'

'She can't possibly feel the same about my baby as I do. She didn't give birth to her. I carried her inside me for nine months. I felt her move. She can't possibly love Hannah the way I do.'

Beth looked at Liz Jackson, who nodded in response to her unspoken question.

'We've got every available person onto it,' she said quietly. 'As you say, whoever has her won't have got far.'

'But surely it can't have been an opportunist snatching? To have taken the baby from the car? Parked so close to the house. . .?'

'No, we think it has to be someone local. Someone who knows the area and who knows Mrs Dawson, probably only from a distance, so to speak, but well enough to have observed her day-to-day movements.'

Neil frowned. 'So you think she may have been watching, saw her chance and seized it. It was a spur-of-the-moment thing?'

'It looks very much like it. I've been assigned to stay with Mrs Dawson as long as she needs me. Besides,' she said in a lowered voice, 'you never know in cases like this—there might be a ransom demand.'

Beth felt the breath catch in her throat. 'Is it likely?'

Liz Jackson shook her head wryly. 'Ransom isn't usually the motive in these cases. Someone wanted a baby desperately enough to take one.'

'Is it. . .is it likely that she'll be harmed?'

'We don't think so, not at this stage. As time goes

on, who knows? The chances are that she won't. I know it's a small consolation but at least it's something, and it's all we have to offer right now.' Her mobile radio crackled into life and she moved away.

'I wish George was here,' Beth said flatly.

'He will be.' Neil's arm tightened round her and she looked up at him.

'I don't know what to do. I need to be doing *something*.' She looked at him. 'How many places are there to hide a baby? There must be somewhere we can look.'

His grip tightened on her shoulders. 'The police are doing all they can, Beth. They're experienced at this sort of thing. Besides, Becky needs you here right now. The baby is too young to know what's happening,' he reasoned. 'If this woman, whoever she is, wanted a baby so desperately then she's going to care for it—'

'Assuming she knows how,' she flung at him. 'How can we be sure?'

'We can't,' he rasped. 'But it won't help the police and it won't help Becky if we assume the worst.'

She knew he was right. For her friend's sake she had to remain calm, but it wasn't easy. She broke away with a sigh of frustration, just as George's car slewed to a halt with a screech of tyres on the drive. White-faced, he headed for the house, pushing past a policeman, then Becky was in his arms.

Half an hour later, having persuaded her to lie down, he came downstairs. He had disposed of his tie and jacket and was chain-smoking. It seemed to Beth as she held him tight that he had aged ten years in the space of one day.

'She's asleep,' George rasped. 'It's the best thing for her. At least she won't know what's going on—for a while, anyway.'

'She'll probably sleep for some time,' Neil said. 'The sedative I gave her was quite strong.'

'I'm grateful to you both.' George's voice broke. 'How could anyone do a thing like this? Why?' He beat his fist against the door. 'I'd like to get my hands around her neck—'

'George.' Beth's hand was on his arm. 'I know how you must feel but the police know what they're doing. You have to let them get on with it. It's all any of us can do.'

'They've talked to the neighbours,' he said flatly.

She nodded. 'And they're making other inquiries. They have a routine for this sort of thing. I know it sounds harsh, cold-blooded even, but it's best to let them get on with it.'

Red-eyed, he looked at her and nodded. 'I know you're right. It's just damned hard.'

'I know.' With an effort she managed a smile. 'I'm Hannah's godmother, you know. Or, at least, I will be.' She embraced him again, waiting until he had gained some semblance of self-control before gently breaking away. 'If there's anything I can do?'

He shook his head, saying gruffly, 'We just want her back, that's all.'

'Would you like me to stay?'

He shook his head again. 'If I'm going to bawl my eyes out I think I'd rather do it in private. There's nothing you can do. The longer Becky sleeps the better. God knows how I'll deal with it later if there isn't any news. I can't think about it.' He looked at them both. 'I'll call you the minute I hear anything.'

Beth's head was throbbing as they walked back out to the car. Her hands shook as she fumbled with the doorhandle, and Neil's hand brushed against hers as he opened it for her.

Ten minutes later they were at the cottage and she climbed out and stood in the dark, waiting for him to drive away. Somewhere along the line the day had vanished. She felt cold and tired and in need of a good cry.

Fumbling for her keys, she faced him. 'Thanks for being here. I'm really grateful. I don't know how I'd have managed. . .'

His glittering gaze narrowed. 'I'm not leaving you, Beth.' He took the keys from her nerveless fingers, stilling her agitated movements as he tilted her chin up and forced her to look at him. 'Did you seriously imagine that I would?'

'You don't have to stay.' Her voice cracked. 'I can cope. I'll be fine.'

'You're not fine. You're far from fine, and if you're going to spend the night in a chair, waiting for the phone to ring, I'm going to be with you. Unless you have some objection, that is?'

A sob caught in her throat as she stared at him bleakly. With one gruff oath, he took her in his arms.

'It's all right, Beth. It's all right.'

'This is ridiculous,' she choked. 'I'm a doctor, for heaven's sake. I'm supposed to be able to cope.'

'Even doctors are human, Beth. They have emotions. It *is* allowed.'

She made a weak attempt to appreciate the joke but he was cradling her head against his chest, surrounding her with his male presence, and suddenly she knew she didn't want to be alone—didn't want him to go.

'What about Jamie?'

'I spoke to Sally and explained. He was going to spend the night there, anyway. There's a school trip tomorrow and they wanted to make an early start. So there's no reason why I can't stay—unless you'd rather

I didn't?' He bent towards her and his mouth found hers, brushing lightly but undemandingly against her lips.

It needed an effort of will to drag her eyelids open as he released her.

'Come on,' he said roughly. 'I think we could both do with some coffee.'

Inside the cottage she headed for the kitchen, flipped the switch on the kettle and made coffee. Neil took his cup and proffered a glass.

'I took the liberty. It's brandy.'

'I can see that. I thought you said coffee.'

'I decided we needed something stronger.'

She looked at him and thought, Right now I need to be in your arms. Her lips trembled. 'I don't like brandy.'

'You've had a shock. It'll make you feel better.'

She took a sip, coughing as the brandy burned its way down her throat, then put the glass down. Neil was right, she thought, huddling to capture some of the heat. She *was* in shock. Only now was she beginning to realise the full enormity of what had happened—of what could still go so tragically wrong.

Taking several deep breaths, she straightened and half turned away, only to feel Neil's hands on her shoulders.

'Hang on, Beth. It's going to be all right.'

She looked at him, her face taut with strain. 'Becky's right. We can't possibly know that.' She tried to break away but his grip merely tightened. 'I heard myself saying all the right things—what I *thought* were the right things—and all the time I was thinking, what if it goes wrong?'

She clasped her arms around her body in a self-protecting embrace. 'There aren't any guarantees, are there? Let's face it. . .' she gave a harsh laugh '. . .we don't even know who we're dealing with.'

His own breathing was ragged as he held her, his hand cupping her chin and forcing her to look at him. 'I know how you feel. Becky is your friend.'

'I doubt if you could even begin to understand what she's going through,' she flung back hotly.

'Of course I understand.' His hands tightened until he was almost shaking her. 'Are you forgetting Jamie? Every parent understands this kind of nightmare.'

She tensed, staring up at him. 'It's not the same.' Her breath caught in her throat. If it were *her* baby. . . There weren't enough words to describe what she would feel. Rage, fear, terror. She knew *exactly* what Becky was going through.

She pressed her hands against his chest, breaking free. 'Why don't they phone?'

'They will,' he said softly, handing her the glass of brandy. This time she drank without protest, almost unaware of its heat, burning her throat as she turned to stare blindly out of the window. 'It's getting late, and it's so cold.'

'Beth.'

'I can't help it.' She blinked hard, glancing over her shoulder at him. 'What makes someone do a thing like this? What sort of person would snatch a baby from its mother?'

'Someone who's very unhappy. Someone desperate—' He broke off and she felt her heart miss a beat as she turned to look at him.

'Neil? What is it? You've thought of something?'

'I'm not sure. It's just an idea.'

'It doesn't matter.' Her hand was on his arm. 'At least it's somewhere to start.'

He frowned. 'You remember shortly after I arrived

here? I discussed a patient with you. I was worried
about her.' He frowned. 'What was her name? Weston?
Walker? Damn it!'

'Wheeler.' She felt her heart give an extra thud.

'That's it. *Grace* Wheeler.' His hands gripped her
arms. 'She was suffering from depression.'

'Yes, I remember. She'd suffered a. . .a stillbirth.'
She stared at him. 'You don't think. . .?'

'I don't know. It's possible. She was certainly
desperate enough.'

'What are you going to do?'

'I'm calling the police.' He strode to the phone and
began dialling. 'I don't have any choice. I know it's
only guesswork but there's nothing else to go on.
Yes. . . It's Dr Quinn here. . .'

From the kitchen where she made more coffee, more
for something to keep her occupied than because she
needed it, she could hear the soft tones of his voice.
He finished the call just as she was returning down the
hall to the sitting room.

'What did they say?'

'It seems Grace Wheeler's name had already been
brought to their attention.' He gave a wry smile.
'Inquiries, as they say, are already under way. Obviously, I didn't give them any confidential details about
her medical history, except that I had a patient who
was extremely depressed and may be in urgent need
of help.

'I've given them this number. They'll call if there's
anything to report. In which case, as her doctor, I may
be needed, anyway.'

'Neil, what if we're wrong?'

'Then no harm's done. The police are simply making
inquiries. But if we're right. . .'

She stared at him, then nodded. Suddenly she felt

very tired and cold. 'And, if we are, what then? What will happen to her?'

'She'll need a lot of help,' he said softly as he put his hands on her shoulders, drawing her slowly towards him. 'She'll get the counselling she needs.'

She frowned. 'Maybe we should have done something more.'

'Like what? We're not miracle-workers, Beth. The patient has to want to be helped. Treating depression without tackling the cause is like dealing with half the problem. Grace Wheeler didn't want help—she wanted tablets.' Frowning, he kissed her gently. 'We both know they aren't the complete answer, but first the patient has to admit there's a problem.'

'That's not always as easy as it sounds.'

'I'm not saying it is. What I'm saying is that we don't always have the answers.'

She swallowed hard on the aching tightness in her throat. 'The crazy thing is that she and Becky had so much in common. They were both desperate for a baby. They would have done anything. Becky just happened to be lucky, that's all.'

His dark brows drew together as he grazed her cheek with his thumb. 'Beth, I don't for one second belittle what Grace Wheeler must have gone through. What happened was tragic and she'll need all the help and support we can give her. But medically there's no reason why she shouldn't one day have a perfectly healthy baby.'

She gave a slight laugh. 'You make it sound so simple.'

'I'm not saying that.' He frowned. 'I'm a doctor. I look for logical answers—' He broke off as the phone began to ring.

Involuntarily, Beth stiffened, her eyes widening with

panic, only to feel the gentle but firm pressure of Neil's hand on her arm.

'It's all right. I'll get it.'

Her fingers shook as she reached for her brandy, glad of its reviving warmth as she listened to the muffled sound of his voice in the hall. When he came back into the room he was smiling, and her heart gave an extra thud.

'It's all right. The baby's been found.'

'Is she. . .?'

'She's safe and well and on her way back to her mum.'

'Oh, thank God.' Without even being aware of it, she was in his arms and he was holding her tight as she wept with the release of so many pent-up emotions. After a few moments she drew away, to say shakily, 'What about Grace Wheeler?'

'From what I gather, she gave the baby up without a struggle. It sounds as if she's in shock. She'll be seen by the duty doctor and I imagine they'll detain her in hospital, for her own safety as much as anything.'

She looked at him and was surprised to find she was still shaking. 'That poor woman. The past few months must have been a nightmare for her.'

'Hey, come on. You're supposed to be glad. Everything's turned out for the best. The baby's back where she belongs.'

Her chin rose. 'Yes, I suppose you're right. I just wish I could believe it's that simple.'

His blue eyes searched her face intently as he touched her cheek. 'Beth, what's wrong? I know you've had a shock, but it's over.' His warm breath was against her hair as he held her. 'There's nothing more for you to worry about.'

She eased herself away to look at him. 'Did you

really believe what you said when you told Becky that the woman who had snatched her baby would take care of it?'

He frowned. 'I haven't come across too many cases of child abduction. I don't have the statistics but usually the woman who carries out the abduction, as in Grace Wheeler's case, is desperate to have a child and treats it as if it *were* her own.' A nerve pulsed in his jaw. 'There are never any guarantees, Beth. You know that as well as I do.'

She shot him a look. 'But Becky was right when she said that no one could love her baby the way she did.'

His face was taut as he looked at her. 'If you're asking about maternal instinct then, yes, I'd say the bond between a mother and her baby is probably the strongest on earth. That's the way it has to be for the human race to survive. I've seen mothers identify the sound of their own baby's cry from a nursery full of protesting infants. I've seen instances of that inbuilt sixth sense a mother seems to get when her child is ill or in danger.'

'So. . .what if that maternal bond doesn't exist?'

He frowned. 'I don't understand what you're trying to say.'

She swallowed hard. 'It's simple enough. What about in cases of. . .adopted children, for instance? Step-children? Foster-children?' She moistened her dry lips with her tongue. 'What you're saying is that the woman's feelings can't be the same because the emotional bond isn't there?'

A spasm flickered briefly across his features. 'Beth, where is this leading? I don't know what you want me to say.'

'I've always wondered, you see.' Tears suddenly burned at the back of her eyelids. She blinked them away, afraid to let him see how vulnerable she was. 'I was adopted. I was two at the time. Oh, I don't remember it, not really.'

Some emotion flared briefly in the depths of his blue eyes. 'I didn't know.'

'There's no reason why you should.'

'What happened? Or would you rather not talk about it?'

'Oh, it wasn't dramatic.' She forced herself to look at him, even gave a slight laugh. 'My adoptive parents weren't able to have children of their own. They'd been down all the usual routes, had all the tests. It seems there was no specific reason why it didn't happen—it just didn't. Finally they decided on adoption, and I needed a home.' Her mouth twisted. 'Hey presto, the magic answer. Everyone was happy.'

'Except that. . .you weren't?' His voice sounded suddenly rough-edged with tension.

Her fingers tightened spasmodically. 'Oh, it was fine to begin with. Yes, I was happy. Until things began to change.'

'Beth.' Neil's hands were on her shoulders. 'You don't have to do this.'

'I think I do.' She evaded him when he would have held her. 'I was five when the miracle happened. Suddenly, after all those years of waiting and trying and the disappointments, my mother discovered that she was pregnant.' Her mouth curved. 'We've both seen it happen, haven't we? Couples trying desperately to have a baby. Nothing happens. They adopt and bingo.' She snapped her fingers. 'The woman conceives.'

'Yes, it can happen. It could be down to a change in hormone levels.' He frowned. 'So you were—what? Six? Seven, when the new baby arrived?'

'Michael. Yes, I was almost seven.' Her voice

seemed to be stuck somewhere in her throat. 'He was a beautiful baby. I loved him. . .still love him. . .dearly.'

Neil's gaze narrowed as he watched the emotions flickering on her face. 'But things changed for *you*?'

'I don't think my parents knew it was happening.' Her voice cracked. 'I'm sure they never knowingly treated us differently. But Michael was their son, you see. He was everything they'd ever wanted. A child of their own. And who can blame them for that?' She gave a slight laugh. 'From then on I began to realise I was different, even though I wasn't sure how or why.'

'Did you know you were adopted?'

She turned to the taut face watching her. 'I found out shortly after Michael was born. I heard. . .I heard my mother talking to someone. I'm not sure who.' She shook her head. 'A friend, maybe. It's not important. I heard her say, "And, of course, Beth is our adopted daughter, you know." '

Neil swore softly under his breath.

'I didn't understand what it meant,' she said softly, drawing a deep breath. 'Shortly after that they told me—explained that I was someone else's baby but they had chosen me specially to be their little girl. I know they meant well but somehow after that I always knew I was second best. Michael was quicker, brighter. His sports days were always more important—' She broke off and gave a wry smile.

'I know all about sibling rivalry. I love Michael, I always have. I just wanted the Maitlands to go on loving me.'

He drew her roughly towards him. 'Don't, Beth.' His fingers laced gently in her hair as he tilted her face to kiss her. 'It's over—in the past. They must have loved you in their own way.'

'But that's it, don't you see?' She shook her head,

pushing weakly against him. 'They loved me *in their own way*. But never quite the way they loved Michael.' Hot colour invaded her cheeks. 'The bond wasn't there. They must have thought it was. *I* thought it was. But then I realised how it *should* be—the way it is with Becky and her baby. It doesn't work without it, don't you see that?'

He relaxed his grip to look at her with narrowed eyes. 'Beth, the Maitlands got it wrong. Can't you see? It doesn't have to be like that for you—for us. This *is* about Jamie, isn't it?'

She drew a ragged breath. 'You said yourself that the maternal bond is stronger than any other. If I. . . we. . .had a baby of our own how—?' She broke off. 'Much as I love Jamie, how can I be sure things wouldn't change? What if I get it wrong?'

'Beth. . .' He reached out for her but she evaded him.

'Don't you see, it's a risk I'm not prepared to take? There's too much at stake. I love you. I *do* love you. Which is why I think it's best, for all our sakes. . .if I don't see you socially again. From now on I'd rather we kept our relationship strictly professional.'

CHAPTER NINE

IN THE week that followed on the surface, at least, the daily routine of the practice went on pretty much as it always had.

At the end of a particularly gruelling day, made worse by the start of what could well turn out to be an epidemic of bronchial flu, Beth climbed into bed feeling both mentally and physically exhausted and praying that she would sleep. An hour and a half later she was still awake, staring into the darkness.

She had never been more glad of the solid routine which, if it didn't keep her mind fully occupied, at least kept her hands busy. And as long as she worked she would survive, she told herself fiercely as she punched her pillow for the tenth time.

Where Neil was concerned, by means of careful avoidance she hadn't seen him, other than at a distance, for several days. With the practice staff run off its feet, it had been surprisingly easy—especially when it seemed he was adopting much the same principle.

She knew she should be grateful he was making things easier than they might otherwise have been yet, perversely, she still found herself looking for him.

The moon went behind a cloud. Perhaps it was time she made a move, too. It wouldn't be easy. Her roots—everything she knew—were here in Wadeley. And so was Neil, her tiny inner voice hammered in her brain. No, things couldn't be allowed to drift on as they were. Sooner or later the inevitable tensions were bound to affect her work and then the practice.

Somewhere there must be another small, out-of-town practice where she could make a comfortable living as a junior partner.

She had fallen asleep with nothing resolved, and the thought was still with her when she woke next morning to a splitting headache and the realisation that she had overslept.

Maybe because she had other things on her mind— or simply because she had been tired—she had forgotten to set the alarm and consequently arrived at the surgery fifteen minutes later than usual, breathless and having had no breakfast other than a strong, black coffee.

Any hopes she might have had of avoiding Neil were dashed as he came out of his consulting room just as she was making her apologies to Ruth and the waiting patients.

Her stomach tightened in a sharp spasm of apprehension before she half turned away, intending to reach for her notes—only to freeze as his image registered in her brain. His appearance shocked her. He looked tired—more than that, he looked drained. His mouth was tight, his blue eyes hard. Beth looked at him sharply. It was a few days since she had seen him and the change in him shocked her.

On the point of walking away, something held her back. It wasn't as if she knew what to say. The only thing she knew for certain was that she felt the distance between them as if it were a tangible thing, and it hurt—even if it was of her own making.

'Remind me to talk to Annie about Mr Harris's diet, will you?' she said to Ruth, before deliberately studying her list of patients with an intensity it didn't warrant.

'Beth, wait. I was hoping to talk to you.'

She hovered at the desk, looking at him warily. Her

emotions were so close to the surface that she wasn't sure she could trust herself to be near him, without letting go and seeing every resolve she had made fall apart. She gave him a remote smile and half turned away.

'I'm sorry. I don't think that's a good idea. I really am busy. Now, if you'll excuse me? Emma. . .' she looked at the girl behind the desk 'can you rustle up Mrs Lever's notes for me? I don't seem to have them and I need to see her later.'

Emma's glance flickered between the two of them. 'I'll make sure they're here for you before you go out again.'

'Thanks.' Beth looked at her watch. 'At this rate I'll still be here at teatime.' She started to walk along the corridor. Neil followed, his expression grim.

'I meant it when I said I needed to talk to you.'

'And I've explained that I really am busy.'

'Don't worry, Doctor. It's business,' he said dryly.

She sighed heavily and came to a halt, almost wishing she hadn't as it brought him tantalisingly closer. 'What's the problem?'

He frowned. 'No problem. I just thought you'd want to know that Grace Wheeler is making progress. She's still in hospital, but at least her medication is being monitored and she's receiving counselling.'

'Oh, that is good news. I'm glad. Will she be charged with the abduction?'

Neil frowned, raking a hand through his hair. 'I imagine so. I'm not sure. But this sort of case is usually dealt with sympathetically.'

'I hope so, for her sake.' She turned away.

'One other piece of good news. Her husband is back. It seems he panicked when they lost the baby through the stillbirth. The family crowded in to give support to

Grace. I think he felt overwhelmed and a bit superfluous. But he's back and seems to want to stay.'

Beth felt the tears of emotion pricking at her eyelids. Instinctively she held out her hand. It was immediately covered by his. 'That's wonderful news. I'm so happy for both of them.'

'Well, at least it proves that things *can* work out for the best. Sometimes there is a happy ending.'

She swallowed hard, seeming to realise for the first time that he was holding her hand. 'Neil, don't, please.'

He drew a harsh breath and released her. 'How's Becky?'

Fine.' With an effort, she forced a smile. 'The baby's thriving. They're all fine. How. . .how's Jamie?'

He frowned. 'A bit off colour.'

She turned to look at him. 'What do you mean? In what way off colour?'

'Oh, you know children.' He shook his head. 'Nothing specific. He woke with a bit of a headache. Probably fancied a day off school. It seemed best not to take any chances. Sally took him over to stay with her.'

'Yes, well. . .'

His mouth tightened. 'Beth, we can't leave things like this. I've been going through hell. We have to talk.'

She stared at him. There was no mistaking the strain on his face, but nothing had changed. Nothing *could* change. Loving them both, as she did, how could she risk hurting them?

'There's nothing to talk about,' she said flatly. 'Please, Neil, don't do this. I won't change my mind.'

He stepped aside, swearing softly as a patient came along the corridor. 'Beth. . .'

But she was already walking away, blinking back the tears as she closed the consulting room door firmly behind her.

Somehow she got through the morning. 'There we are, Mr Davies.' Beth smiled sympathetically as she handed over a prescription. 'These tablets should help to get rid of the migraine. They're fast-acting, which is the main thing, and they should help to ease the queasy tummy too.'

Andy Davies smiled weakly as he rose to his feet. Forty, tall and if anything slightly underweight, he folded the slip of paper carefully into the pocket of his neatly tailored suit.

'I can't understand why it happened now.' He adjusted the set of his glasses on his nose. 'I haven't had an attack for a couple of years. I thought I'd got over the damned things. It would have to happen now, of all times.'

Beth smiled as she also rose to her feet. 'Yes, well, that may be the clue. You said you started the new job about three months ago.'

He gave a slight laugh. 'I was lucky to get it, especially at my age.'

She smiled. 'Forty is hardly old.'

'It is when there are kids fresh out of university, clutching their degrees and snapping at your heels.' He laughed wryly and winced. 'I was out of work for over a year. It came as a shock. This new job was a life-saver, I don't mind telling you. Trouble is, there's no nine to five any more, is there?'

'I know what you mean.' She laughed with him. 'Even so, you need to ease up a bit.'

'I'll tell the boss that when I see him. I'm sure he'll be pleased.'

She was seeing the last of her patients out, a couple of hours later. 'I'll see you next week then, Mrs Smith. Try the cream until then and we'll see how it goes. If there's no real improvement we'll try something else.'

Returning to her room, she checked her diary, made a couple of phone calls and then made her way to Reception where Ruth was talking on the phone. Handing over the cards, Beth looked at her watch.

'I've only got one call and that isn't urgent so I thought I'd pop back to the cottage first to grab a sandwich and a cup of coffee.' Along with a couple of aspirins, she thought, briefly kneading the throbbing at her temple. 'Oh, and if the day hospital calls will you tell them I've arranged for Mrs Broadstone to go in on Thursdays? She's happier with that. So we need transport to pick her up.'

'Will do.' Emma glanced out of the window. 'It looks as if we're in for some more rain.'

'Typical! I'm sure someone up there knows when it's my half-day off. Anyway, I'll see you.' With a wave, Beth headed for the door.

'Oh, Dr Maitland, there's a call for you.' Ruth's voice brought her to a halt with a sigh of impatience.

'Is it urgent?' she mouthed. 'Can you take a message?'

Ruth covered the receiver with a hand. 'It's a Mrs Prentiss.'

'Prentiss? Oh, you mean *Sally* Prentiss, the childminder.' Beth frowned. 'But don't you want Neil?'

Ruth shook her head. 'She asked for you.'

Beth took the phone. 'Hello? Yes, Beth Maitland. Yes, of course I do. Only don't you want—? Oh, and you've tried his mobile? No, no, that is odd. Just hold on a second. Ruth? Have you any idea where Neil was heading?'

Ruth shook her head. 'Not really. He left about. . . half an hour ago. I know he had several calls.'

'Right, thanks. Hello? Well, he's definitely out on a call somewhere. Yes. Jamie. . .?' She frowned. 'Are

you worried about him? You're not. Yes, Neil mentioned this morning that Jamie had a headache. Has he
been sick?' She looked at her watch.

'Well, look, I'm on my way back to the cottage. If
you haven't managed to contact Neil fairly soon and
you start to feel worried then call me again at home.
No, of course it's no trouble. You did absolutely the
right thing.'

'Problem?' Ruth asked as Beth handed back
the phone.

'It's Jamie. Neil mentioned earlier that he was a bit
off colour.'

Ruth smiled. 'It's probably nothing serious. You
know what kids are. Up one minute, down the next.'

'Yes, I expect you're right.' Beth smiled. 'Sally
Prentiss is pretty level-headed. She has two boys of her
own so I'm sure if she was worried she'd say so. Look,
I'm going back to the cottage. If you hear from Neil
in the meantime. . .'

'Don't worry. I'll put him in the picture.'

Ten minutes later Beth was back at the cottage. Having let Henry out, she made herself a sandwich and
decided to make the most of her afternoon off. She ran
herself a bath and add a generous amount of her favourite bath oil, before lying back and allowing the warm
water to soothe away her weariness and tensions.

Except that she found herself thinking about Jamie
instead. She frowned. He was usually such a lively little
boy that it was unlike him to be out of sorts. It was
probably a bug of some kind. There were certainly
plenty of them around. All the same, she would have
felt happier if they had been able to contact Neil.

Stifling a sigh, she climbed out of the bath and dried
herself vigorously on a towel. A few minutes later,
dressed in jeans and a warm sweater, she slipped her

feet into a pair of well-worn trainers and made herself a strong cup of black coffee. Glancing at the rapidly fading afternoon light, she made a series of phone calls.

She knew she was probably worrying unnecessarily, but it wasn't like Neil not to stay in touch. Fifteen minutes later, as she was feeding Henry, the phone rang. It was Sally Prentiss and she sounded worried.

'Sally, I thought when I didn't hear from you that everything was all right.'

'I wish it was. Beth, I still haven't been able to contact Neil and I'm getting a bit worried about Jamie. He isn't any better. In fact, I'd say he's slightly worse. I've spoken to Ruth again, but there's still no word from Neil.'

Beth frowned, experiencing her first real pang of alarm. 'No, I rang the surgery myself a while ago. Look, I've done some checking. I've gone through his list of calls and managed to contact most of them by phone to confirm that he was actually there. He's probably between calls somewhere, but he still isn't answering his mobile.'

She tried to dismiss the sudden qualm that rippled through her, but it wasn't that easy. Neil should have finished his calls by now, shouldn't he? She glanced at her watch. It would be dark soon. The roads were still icy. What if there had been an accident?

She pushed the thought away. 'It could just be that his mobile is faulty.'

'Yes, I was thinking that.' The uncertainty in Sally Prentiss's voice was palpable.

'Are you still concerned about Jamie?'

'Yes. I'm probably worrying unnecessarily, but I think he's getting worse, Beth. I've given him a dose of Calpol but, if anything, I'd say his temperature is up since I last spoke to you.' She gave a slight laugh. 'Which probably explains why he's so irritable.'

Beth couldn't get rid of the sudden tight feeling in her chest. 'Look, how about if I pop over and take a look at him?'

'Would you?' There was an audible sigh of relief from the other end of the phone. 'I'm sorry to panic but—'

'I'll be with you in fifteen minutes.'

She made it in twelve. 'Where is Jamie?'

'Upstairs.' Sally was already leading the way. 'He seems very sleepy, and he's been sick again.'

'Any word from Neil yet?'

'No. Ruth knows the situation. She's going to keep trying to contact him.'

'Well, try not to worry. I'm sure he's simply been held up. He'll finish his calls soon.'

Jamie was lying on the bed. His eyes were closed and his small face was flushed. Beth put her briefcase down, slipped off her jacket and sat beside him.

'Hello, Jamie.' Smiling, she took one small hand in her own.

Fretfully he turned his head to look at her. 'Beff. I wanted you to come. I was waiting.'

Looking at him, she felt her heart give an odd little lurch. 'Auntie Sally tells me you're not feeling very well. Can you tell me where it hurts?'

One small hand drifted weakly in the direction of his head.

'And what about your neck?' Very gently, disturbing him as little as possible, she made as thorough an examination as she could and felt her spirits sink.

'Jamie, I wonder if you could do something for me. Can you try to sit up and bend your knees?' She helped him as he struggled lethargically to move. 'Now, can you kiss your knees?' She watched as he tried to do as she asked, whimpering fretfully. 'It's all right, darling. You did very well. Lie back now and rest.'

'You won't go away, will you, Beff?'

'No, I won't leave you, Jamie.' Glancing at Sally, she moved away from the bed and said quietly, 'When did you last take his temperature?'

'Just after I spoke to you. It was thirty-one degrees.'

'And you say he's been sick?'

Sally nodded, her attractive face anxious. 'Beth, what is it?'

'You just rest, Jamie.' Beth leaned forward to kiss the flushed cheek. 'We're going to try to make you feel better.'

'Daddy?'

'He'll be here very soon.' Please, God, she thought. Where are you, Neil? Suddenly the only thing in the world she wanted was to see him walk through the door.

Her heart was thudding as she rose to her feet, gathering up her briefcase, and they made their way quietly downstairs.

'It's serious, isn't it?' Sally looked at Beth, her face pale with apprehension.

'I think it might be.' Beth's own voice was taut. 'He's very drowsy and irritable. The high temperature is worrying, and there's definite spinal stiffness. I gather he's been a bit off colour recently?'

'Well, he had a bit of a sore throat. Most of the kids have, but they seemed to get over it. Why?'

Beth opened her briefcase and hunted for her mobile phone. She knew the colour had drained from her own face. 'Look, I'm going to call for an ambulance. I want to get Jamie admitted to hospital as soon as possible. I can't be absolutely certain until they've done some tests but. . .I think it may be meningitis.'

'Oh, my God!'

Beth was already tapping out the number. Where was Neil? 'The ambulance is on its way,' she confirmed seconds later.

'What can I do? There must be something. I feel so useless.'

'The main thing is to stay calm.' Easier said than done, Beth thought as her own heartbeat suddenly seemed to settle into a higher gear. 'Where are the twins?'

'Over at my sister's. We were all going over there for the day, then Jamie wasn't too well so she took the boys with her.' Sally's eyes widened in sudden panic. 'My God, the twins. Isn't meningitis catching?'

'It can be. It depends on the type, and we won't know that until the hospital have done all the tests.' Beth put an arm round the other woman's shoulders. 'If it is the contagious variety then the twins, and any-one else who's been in close contact with Jamie, will be given antibiotics as a precautionary measure. But if the boys seem healthy—'

She broke off with an audible gasp of relief as a car suddenly came to a halt on the drive and a door slammed.

'Neil!'

His voice was taut as they opened the door to let him in. 'What's happening? I got a message from Ruth to get in touch urgently.'

Sally said, 'We've been trying to contact you on your mobile but we couldn't get any answer.'

His mouth tightened. 'I left it in the car while I went to visit Mr Peters up at the nursing home. When I got back to the car the window had been smashed and the phone was gone. What's wrong with Jamie? Where is he?'

'He's upstairs.' Instinctively, Beth reached out and took his hand.

'Beth, what is it? I have to know.'

She swallowed hard. 'Neil, I can't be sure but. . .I think it may be meningitis. The ambulance is on its way.'

Even as she spoke, flashing blue lights heralded its arrival. Neil drew a harsh breath as he looked at her in stunned disbelief. '*Meningitis*!'

'I could be wrong.'

He gave her one quick look. 'I trust your judgement. Dear God, if he. . . If anything happens. . .'

Sally let the ambulance crew in. Minutes later, Jamie was being settled into the ambulance.

'I'm coming with you.' Beth was already following as Neil strode away. 'You go with him. I'll follow in my car and meet you there.' His hand briefly squeezed her arm.

The drive to the hospital seemed interminable, conscious as she was of what Neil must be going through — of the emotions that must be seething through him as he feared for his son's life.

She shared every moment of his anguish. If she could have done anything to lessen it she would have done it, but there was nothing either of them could do to banish the nightmare except wait and pray.

She was driving too fast, though she was hardly aware of it until the car hit a patch of ice on the road.

Gasping, she was flung forward and she had to take several deep breaths after she'd fought to bring the car back under control. Minutes later she climbed, shivering, out of the car as the ambulance doors swung open and Jamie was lifted out gently but expertly.

Nursing staff were waiting to meet them. Beth's hand tightened briefly over Neil's arm. He held Jamie's hand as they walked the seemingly endless length of the corridors.

'We'll need to isolate him for a while,' Sister Mary McBride, tall, dark-haired and attractive in her blue uniform, said as she briskly led the way. 'Until the diagnosis is established. Mr Saunders will examine him and he'll need to carry out some tests.'

Doors opened and swung soundlessly closed.

'We want to be with him,' Neil insisted, and Beth silently blessed him for his inclusion of her.

They were led into a small room where the medical team took over—efficient, capable—going through a process they had gone through so many times that their actions were automatic.

'He's very restless. Have the cot sides ready, will you, Nurse?' The instructions were quietly given as Sister McBride eased off Jamie's clothing, causing him as little disturbance as possible.

Brian Saunders, who was sixty years old, tall and grey-haired, spoke quietly to Neil as he made his preliminary examination.

'I know it looks pretty awful, and I can imagine what you must both be going through. Meningitis strikes so quickly and out of the blue, which makes it all the more frightening. But you did the right thing, getting here as fast as you did. Time is vital in cases like this.'

Beth felt the pressure of Neil's hand tighten briefly on her arm as she watched, wondering if it was all part of some nightmare she had accidentally wandered into. She had seen it all before so many times, but somehow this was different. It was Neil's son lying there, baby limbs splayed, his eyes closed, face flushed. Totally, utterly vulnerable.

'We'll need nose and throat swabs, Sister,' Brian Saunders said quietly. 'Observe his level of conscious-

ness and we'll have temperature, pulse and respirations
done half-hourly.'

He looked at Neil. 'We'll need to do a lumbar puncture. While we wait for the results we'll be starting him
on ampicillin. Once we know for sure what we're up
against we may change that.'

Beth was aware of Neil's distraught face as he briefly
held his son's hand, so tiny in his own larger one. She
wasn't sure how long they stood there as everything
went on around them. She only knew as she glanced
out of the window that darkness had already fallen,
without either of them even realising it.

She held Jamie's other hand, her fingers moving convulsively. She choked back a small sob, her mind
exhausted—shattered by the fear that they might lose
this small scrap of life before she had a chance to let
him know how much she loved him.

She reached out for Neil's hand, offering silent support. His fingers gripped hers, then his arm closed round
her. They were supporting each other.

'You'll both need somewhere quiet to wait. I know
it's not going to be easy but for now it's best we do
what we have to do,' Brian Saunders was saying as he
led them through to a small side-room, his own face
showing quiet sympathy.

Beth's head ached. She sat in a chair. Someone
brought them coffee in disposable cups. It looked hot
and strong and tasted of nothing but they drank it,
anyway.

Brian Saunders sat in the chair opposite them, frowning as he looked at them both. 'I do have some idea of
what you must be going through,' he said quietly. 'I'd
like to be able to tell you that Jamie is out of danger, but
you know that isn't the case. He does have meningitis.'

He said it as if there might still be some lingering

doubt in their minds. 'As doctors, you'll know there are accompanying risks to the disease. In some cases we get convulsions or even cardiac arrest. But those are the most severe cases.'

Beth knew she was trembling and she felt Neil's hand tighten over hers.

'I couldn't bear it if I lost him,' he rasped. He looked haggard. His face was pale and there was a faint line of stubble on his chin.

'We're not going to lose him,' Beth said with quiet determination. 'We're going to fight this together, and we're going to win.'

Brian Saunders looked at them both. 'I know it probably isn't much of a consolation right now but, from what I've seen so far and from my initial examination of Jamie, I'm as sure as I can be at this stage that he has *viral* meningitis. It's the less severe form of the illness. There's no rash, which is characteristic of bacterial meningitis. If it was going to appear we'd see it by now.'

Beth heard Neil's soft intake of breath. A bleeper sounded and Brian Saunders rose regretfully to his feet. 'Obviously, we'll have to wait a while for the results of the lumbar puncture, but I expect them to confirm what I've just told you. Jamie will need to stay in isolation for a while, usually twenty-four hours. Maybe more, maybe less. We'll keep him comfortable and quiet and we'll be able to keep an eye on him.'

Neil frowned. 'We'd like to spend some time with him.'

'Yes, of course, although I'm sure I don't need to stress the importance of letting Jamie rest.' Brian Saunders smiled wryly as his bleeper sounded again and he moved towards the door. 'I'm wanted on the ward. Look, by all means, pop in and see Jamie as soon as the staff have got him settled. But after that I'd suggest that you both go home and get some sleep. Come in again whenever you want. Meanwhile, if there's any change Sister will call you.'

The door closed quietly behind him. Neil stood at the window, staring into the darkness. Beth stared into the dregs of her coffee, drained it and tossed the paper cup into the bin.

'I can't believe this is happening. I feel as if I'm going to wake up any second now and find it's all been a dream,' she said flatly.

Neil turned slowly to look at her, his face taut. 'I'll never be able to thank you for what you did—for getting him here so promptly.'

She tried to speak but couldn't. Her throat felt too tight. Somehow she was in Neil's arms and they were hugging each other, drawing warmth and comfort from the fact that they were together.

'I can't leave,' he said flatly. 'I have to be here in case. . .'

'He's going to be all right. We have to believe that.'

He glanced down at her. 'You don't have to do this, you know.'

She had to force herself to speak through the tightness in her throat. 'Are you telling me you'd rather I wasn't here?'

'I'm saying you don't have to stay for my sake.'

But what better reason could there be? 'I want to stay,' she said shakily. 'I realise now just how much Jamie means to me. If anything happened. . .'

His own throat tightened in painful spasms. 'If he can get through the next few hours. . .'

But those hours seemed like an eternity as they sat in the small, quiet room. Occasionally they would tiptoe together into the ward where Jamie lay with one small light above the bed illuminating him. It seemed, if anything, to emphasise his vulnerability.

Jamie moved restlessly, unaware of their presence as they kept vigil. From time to time a nurse came into the room and smiled briefly and sympathetically in their direction as she checked monitors and took Jamie's pulse, before quietly leaving them alone again.

It was dawn, and the first pale rays of light were beginning to brighten the sky when Beth rose silently to her feet and went to stare out of the window.

Behind her Neil sat, hunched forward, his head in his hands. She went to him, putting an arm around his shoulders. He reached up, his hand closing over hers.

'Do you want some coffee?' she said softly.

He rose stiffly to his feet, rubbing at his eyes. 'What I need is for someone to walk through that door and tell me that Jamie's taken a turn for the better.' His hand rasped briefly against the stubble on his chin. 'How long is it since we last looked in?'

Her own face was taut with strain. 'Fifteen minutes.'

He gave a ragged sigh. 'I can't believe this night will ever be over.'

'It'll soon be light,' she told him. 'It's snowing again.'

His arms closed round her. She rested her head against his chest as they rocked gently together before she broke away gently.

'I think I'll go and get that coffee. We could both use some.'

Ten minutes later, having taken time to rinse her face in cold water, she returned to the room with two disposable cups of coffee. The room was empty.

She stood, frozen, in the doorway, feeling a sense of panic well up. Something had happened. Jamie must have taken a turn for the worse or Neil would be here.

She almost spilled the coffee in her haste to put it down on the table, before heading almost at a run for the ward. Her heart was pounding. Please, God, don't let us lose him, not now. It isn't fair.

Breathing hard, she pushed the door open and came to a halt as she saw Neil standing by the bed. She had to moisten her dry lips with her tongue before she could speak.

'What is it? What's happened?'

'Nothing. It's all right.' He reached out wearily to gather her to him. 'I just had to see him. I can't sit around, doing nothing. I feel so bloody useless.'

'I know, I know.' Her arm tightened around his waist as she looked up at him, her own breathing ragged as he held her. 'Is there any change?'

He sighed. 'I'm not sure. I thought he seemed to be breathing more easily. But maybe I'm just seeing what I want to see.'

'He doesn't look quite so flushed.' She brushed a hand gently against Jamie's forehead and he stirred restlessly. She frowned. 'Neil, I'm sure his temperature is down.'

She felt the muscles in his arms tense as he moved slightly closer to the bed to brush his own fingers gently against his son's cheek. 'I think you're right.' He drew a harsh breath. 'If the fever's broken maybe he's turned the corner.'

Beth wanted to weep at the note of hope in his voice. She wanted to hold him, hold them both, these people she loved. To take away all the hurt and pain.

Her hand reached up to touch Neil's cheek. He looked awful. In the artificial light his features looked haggard. She could only guess how she must look.

'He got through the night, Neil,' she whispered. 'That has to be good.'

'I don't know how I would have borne it without you,' he rasped, his hand stroking her cheek. 'Thank you for staying.'

She looked up at him. There was so much she wanted to say, but where to start? Had she left it too late?

'Daddy?'

The voice was faint but it was there, not a figment of their imagination.

She felt Neil's arm tense. Her own eyes filled with tears of wonderment and she blinked hard. Then they were both moving closer to the small figure on the bed.

'Jamie?' His voice cracking with emotion, Neil was holding his son's small hand and brushing back the damp fair hair. 'Hello, tiger. How are you feeling?'

Jamie moved restlessly before his eyes fluttered open again. 'Auntie Beff?'

'It's all right, darling. I'm here. We're both here.' Her voice seemed to be stuck somewhere in her throat as she looked at Neil and whispered, 'He recognises us. I think he's going to be all right.'

Neil blinked hard, putting his arm around her as he looked at his son. 'You're going to be all right, Jamie. You've been poorly, but you're going to be fine now.'

Restlessly, Jamie flung an arm against his brow before he slowly opened his eyes again, struggling to focus on them.

'You won't go away, will you?' he said plaintively.

'No, Jamie, I won't go away.'

Eyes closed, Jamie nodded. 'I want Auntie Beff to stay, too. I love Auntie Beff.'

She felt Neil's hand tighten spasmodically over hers as he looked at his son, before lifting his head to gaze questioningly into her eyes. He must have read her unspoken answer there because she heard his soft intake of breath before he said quietly, 'I love Beth too, Jamie, and I want her to stay, if she will.'

She felt her eyes fill with tears. She nodded, for a moment unable to speak, then said chokingly, 'For as long as you want me to.'

A nurse came in at that moment, took one look at their faces and moved towards the bed. Gently but expertly she made the routine checks then straightened, smiling.

'I think he's going to be all right,' she pronounced. 'I'll get Mr Saunders to take a look at him, but I think we can safely say the worst is over. Your son is going to be fine, Dr Quinn.'

Two hours later, having seen Jamie settled, they were on their way home. Beth was never quite sure how they got there. She felt dazed with tiredness and excitement, Her emotions seemed to be in turmoil yet somehow they were suddenly in Neil's kitchen, drinking coffee and talking.

'I don't ever want to go through a nightmare like that again,' she murmured.

In the warmth of the sitting room, with snow falling outside the window, neither of them made any move to get on with a new day. It was as if, for the past twenty-four hours, they had been caught up in some kind of time warp. For now the glow from the fire was enough, enclosing them both in its circle of warmth.

Raising his head slowly to look at her, Neil said quietly, 'I meant what I said, you know. I'll never be able to thank you for what you did.'

'I don't need thanks.'

Suddenly, as they faced each other, she found herself wondering where they went from here. It was crazy but suddenly she felt very shy, which was ridiculous when she loved this man so much that just to be near him made her legs feel weak. Her voice faltered. 'Neil, I. . .'

His own breathing was harsh and uneven as he came slowly towards her and put his arms round her. 'I don't think I can let you off so lightly,' he rasped, 'when I think how close I came to losing Jamie. If you hadn't done what you did—as quickly as you did—'

'Don't!' Her fingers rose to touch his lips. She didn't want to think what might have happened. She looked up at him, her eyes glistening with tears. 'He's going to be all right. He *is*. That's all that matters.'

He looked down at her. 'You do realise what you're saying?'

Her throat tightened and she said huskily, 'If you mean do I want you and Jamie as part of my life, then, yes. I should have realised it sooner. I *did* realise. I was just fighting against it.'

She stirred in his arms, revelling in the loving warmth of him. She could feel his heart thudding beneath his shirt.

'We were going to talk,' he said.

'There's so much to say. I'm not sure I know where to start. I seem to have made so many mistakes.' Her voice was muffled as he held her close. 'I'm not sure I can explain. . .'

'Don't, Beth.' His fingers brushed against her mouth, silencing the words, Then, before she knew what was happening, his mouth came down on hers—relentless, firm, demanding.

They clung together, Beth offering no resistance as his hands moved over her body. He raised his head briefly to look down at her.

'I love you,' he groaned softly as his mouth made feathery advances over her throat, lips and eyes and then back to her mouth, claiming it with a fierce possession that left them both breathless.

She responded with a ferocity that matched his own, filled with a need to hold him—to be part of him in the only way she knew how.

'I need you in my life, Beth. I never stop thinking about you or worrying about you.' His voice faltered as he saw the confusion in her eyes.

She had to force herself to speak through the tightness in her throat. 'Maybe I've been too busy thinking about my own needs to think about anyone else's,' she murmured huskily. Within a matter of hours a whole lot of her values seemed to have changed.

His breathing was uneven as he glanced down at her. 'And just what are your needs, Beth?'

She felt the sudden surge of warm colour in her cheeks. 'Right now, all I know is that my life wouldn't seem complete without you—and Jamie—in it,' she said brokenly. 'I've been confused about a lot of things. I've had doubts, but they weren't about you—or Jamie, I realise that now. They were about me. Somewhere along the way a lot of things seem to have got mixed up.'

'We can sort it all out,' he grated. 'I don't think I'll ever be able to let you go again.'

'I wouldn't want you to,' she said unevenly. 'I love you, too.'

He cupped her chin, looking down at her tenderly but still with a hint of the anguish he'd been through in his eyes. 'You do know where this is leading? You know what I'm saying?'

'I think so,' she said softly as she met his gaze. 'You yourself said that Jamie is part of you so how could I *not* love him? I know Jamie will always be Louise's son,' Her voice cracked. 'But I'd like to think she might have wanted someone else to love him the way she did. *Exactly* the way she did, I know now that I can. I've been such a fool, wasted so much time.'

He said gently, his throat tightening in painful spasms, 'You've been hurt. I can understand.'

'You were hurt, too, when you lost Louise. I realise what she must have meant to you, but you got on with your life. I just wasn't sure. . .' She frowned. 'I wasn't sure there would ever be room for me. . .'

Neil groaned. 'Oh, my darling. I can't say I didn't love Louise. I did. She'll always be part of my life, the part that gave me Jamie.

But what *we* have—it's different, don't you see? I feel I've been given a second chance at happiness, and I want to grab it with both hands.'

Beth swallowed hard. 'It was more complicated.'

His finger gently grazed her cheek as he looked at her. 'Because of Jamie, you mean?'

'Because my feelings. . .about children. . .about how I would cope were all mixed up.' She looked up at him. 'My parents might have made a few mistakes, but I've made some, too—some big ones.' She drew a long, shaky breath.

'Maybe I've learned something from them. Maybe I can avoid making the same mistakes. What I do know is that I couldn't love Jamie more if he were my own. I love you both.'

His blue eyes searched her face intently. 'I'd say that was a good basis for working most things out, don't you?'

She whispered, 'You realise you might be taking a risk? How can I be sure. . .?'

His mouth touched hers, tenderly possessive. '*I'm* sure.'

She had to force herself to speak through the tightness in her throat. 'I seem to have wasted so much time. When I think how close I came to losing you—to throwing everything away.'

A groan rose from deep in his throat. His arms tightened round her as though he couldn't bear to let her go and he kissed her again hungrily. 'I don't give up so easily, Beth.' His voice was deep and gritty. 'You may as well start getting used to the idea that Jamie and I are going to be around for a long, long time.'

'It sounds good to me,' Beth stared up at him earnestly.

'It's a lifetime commitment,' His lips moved against hers. 'Are you sure? Really sure?'

She gazed up at him. 'Yes, she whispered. 'Until now I've always felt something was missing in my life.' She had to force herself to speak through the constriction in her throat. 'For the first time in my life I feel as if everything has suddenly slotted into place. I don't feel second best any more. I feel complete, whole. Can you understand that?'

He gazed down at her, his incredibly blue eyes glittering with desire. 'It's only the beginning, Beth. There's so much more.'

'As long as we're together that's all that matters.'

He kissed her, and this time he was more demanding. 'Shall we go and see Jamie?' he rasped as he broke away. 'Before this gets completely out of hand?'

She moved closer, teasing him with the softness of her body against his taut maleness. 'Have I told you lately that I love you, Dr Quinn?'

'Not for at least five minutes,' He looked at her, his mouth slanted. 'You'll have to do better, Dr Maitland.'

Her breath snagged in her throat as he stroked her hair and his mouth brushed her forehead. 'Oh, I intend to,' she whispered, her gaze meeting his with glittering anticipation.

MILLS & BOON®

Medical Romance™

COMING NEXT MONTH

PRECIOUS OFFERINGS by Abigail Gordon

Springfield Community Hospital ... meeting old friends

Rafe was sure that Lucinda couldn't be immune to his charm; after all she was only human; now all he had to do was get her to admit it!

DR McIVER'S BABY by Marion Lennox

Kids & Kisses ... another heart-warming story

Marriage of convenience was definitely the wrong word. Looking after Tom, his baby and his two dogs, Annie thought it must be madness—or was it love?

A CHANCE IN A MILLION by Alison Roberts

It was ancient history. The last time that Fee had seen Jon Fletcher he'd been about to get married and live on the other side of the world. But now he was back and minus a wife...

SOMETHING SPECIAL by Carol Wood

Sam had only one thought on the subject of career women—avoid them at all cost! But getting to know Paula, he was beginning to think he may have been wrong.

On Sale from **4th May 1998**

DEBBIE MACOMBER

The Playboy and the Widow

A confirmed bachelor, Cliff Howard wasn't prepared to
trade in the fast lane for car pools. Diana Collins lived life
hiding behind motherhood and determined to play it
safe. They were both adept at playing their roles.
Until the playboy met the widow...

"Debbie Macomber's stories sparkle with love and laughter..."
—*New York Times* bestselling author, Jayne Ann Krentz

1-55166-080-6
AVAILABLE FROM MAY 1998

MIRA®

DANCE FEVER

How would you like to win a year's supply of Mills & Boon® books? Well you can and they're FREE! Simply complete the competition below and send it to us by 31st October 1998. The first five correct entries picked after the closing date will each win a year's subscription to the Mills & Boon series of their choice. What could be easier?

OBLARMOL
AMBUR
RTOXTFO
RASQUE
GANCO

KOPLA
OOOOMTLCIN
MALOENCF
SITWT
LASSA

EVJI
TAZLW
ACHACH
SCDIO
MAABS

G	R	I	H	C	H	A	R	J	T	O	N
O	P	A	R	L	H	U	B	P	I	B	W
M	O	O	R	L	L	A	B	M	C	V	H
B	L	D	I	O	O	K	C	L	U	P	E
R	K	U	B	N	C	R	Q	H	V	R	Z
S	A	N	I	O	O	N	G	W	A	S	V
T	S	I	N	R	M	G	E	U	B	G	H
W	L	G	H	S	O	R	Q	M	M	B	L
I	A	P	N	O	T	S	L	R	A	H	C
S	S	L	U	K	I	A	S	F	S	L	S
T	O	R	T	X	O	F	O	X	T	R	F
G	U	I	P	Z	N	D	I	S	C	O	Q

D8C

Please turn over for details of how to enter ⇨

HOW TO ENTER

There is a list of fifteen mixed up words overleaf, all of which when unscrambled spell popular dances. When you have unscrambled each word, you will find them hidden in the grid. They may appear forwards, backwards or diagonally. As you find each one, draw a line through it. Find all fifteen and fill in the coupon below then pop this page into an envelope and post it today. Don't forget you could win a year's supply of Mills & Boon® books—you don't even need to pay for a stamp!

**Mills & Boon Dance Fever Competition
FREEPOST CN81, Croydon, Surrey, CR9 3WZ**
EIRE readers send competition to PO Box 4546, Dublin 24.

**Please tick the series you would like to receive if you
are one of the lucky winners**

Presents™ ❏ Enchanted™ ❏ Medical Romance™ ❏
Historical Romance™ ❏ Temptation® ❏

Are you a Reader Service™ subscriber?   Yes ❏   No ❏

Ms/Mrs/Miss/Mr ....Intials ....
(BLOCK CAPITALS PLEASE)

Surname...

Address ....

....

....Postcode.........................

(I am over 18 years of age)   D8C